A Little Red Ridinghood Retelling

BOOK THREE

OKAMI

NICOLETTE
ANDREWS

Dedicated to all my Kickstarter backers who made this book possible! Thanks for believing in me.

This Edition Made Possible By My Kickstarter Backers

Extra Special Thanks To:

Iris, Shireen Harrison, Rebekah Deats, Effie Hofer & Evelynn Hofer, Nathalie, JasZ, Alicia T. Stoesser, & Bryan Zeitz

And Thanks To:

Brittnay King, Li Cai Haney, Ashley Tomlinson, Wendy Alvarez, Lilian, Kara Stogsdill, Kellie N., Megyn "Crimson" MacDougall, Lauren Armstrong, Sunny Side Up, T.L. Branson, Vera Soroka, Tessonja Odette, Kristen White, Allyson Lindt, Matthea W. Ross, Cassidy, Melissa Williams, Billye Herndon, Courtney G, Carlye Pierce, Jenna Leavitt, Foxz Bambina, Charis Lavoie, Taylor Lust, Michelle Huang, Emma Radovich, Michelle Badillo, Katherine Shipman, Hannah Schindler, Kayla Cotrell, Ariadna, Natasha McGrath, Crystal Christian, Oliver Gross, Mekomiya, Melanie Briggs, B. Sawyer, Renee Portnell, Dragondariu, Ursula Urrutia, Ashley Jean, Vixen Rue-Aurora, Alexandra Werhan, Kanyon Kiernan, Iris Pleitez, Melanie Karsak, Stephanie Meredith, Meredith Carstens, Heather Dianne, Catherine Banks, Nikole C., Alli Tambaoan, PunkARTchick *Ruthenia*, Zack Newcomb, Sherry Mock, Charity Chimni, Anna Sherles, Mike Dobey, Chris Munroe, Felicia MacLaren, Manon Lanzarotti, Christina Hecht, Reina Setsuna, Konvinna S., Christina B., Lauren Sarsby, Kris B., Sabrina Elizabeth Cline, Nicole Akeroyd-Slater, Alexandrea M, Myranda Haarman, Robert & Sierra Krusmark

ONE

Shin leaped over a fallen tree. The strong scent of plant decay tickled his nose. Mixed in with it was something unexpected, the musky scent of another wolf. He slowed and lifted his nose to better catch the scent on the wind. The collar around his neck weighed against him, but in the centuries as Akio's slave, he'd learned to account for it.

It couldn't be. The few remaining okami packs were located farther to the north. Being weakened by war and isolation after the fall of the dragon, they kept mostly to their territory. They wouldn't risk venturing into the domain of a powerful yokai like Akio, not by accident. Could it be the dragon had recruited them? When Akio had learned of his return, he'd sent Shin to taunt him. It was a reminder that even centuries later he still owned Shin. Could this okami be the dragon's reply?

Duty calls. Shin sighed. Hopefully some hapless wolf had wandered too far from home. Their scent was strongest along the forest path but quickly diverged into the woods. Other than the smell, there was no other sign of the strange wolf. No prints, no hair, nothing. It was as if a spirit moved through the forest. *I guess it's safe to rule out a lost traveler. Just what I needed...*

Deeper into the forest he followed the strange wolf's trail, where the sun struggled to push through the canopy and the darkness swallowed everything. Fog cloaked the forest floor and obscured his vision. But Shin knew this place well and he could navigate it with his eyes closed.

The trail went cold along a river bank. The fog rolled back and revealed a single human footprint in the mud. Shin pressed his nose against it.

The stink of wolf was all over it. A female wolf. *What are you doing here, I wonder?* Judging by the break in the fog, she wasn't far away either.

An arrow flew past him.

Missing him by a hair, it embedded itself into a nearby tree and wobbled. Shin growled and ruffled the hairs on his back, scanning the surrounding forest for the intruder.

"Come out, you coward. Enough games," he snarled.

A figure stepped out from behind a tree nearby. She wore the red and white of a priestess. Her braided brown hair hung down her back and had been hidden beneath a straw hat. Over her shoulder, she carried a quiver of arrows, and one was nocked, pointed straight at Shin.

He sniffed the air. This was the wolf he'd been following. A wolf in priestess garb? Now he'd seen it all.

Shin transformed from wolf to man and held up his hands. "Hold. There's no need for violence." He wasn't about to fight a fellow okami, especially if she was working for the dragon.

"You were following me," she responded.

She turned her head, tracking him as he inched around trying to get a better look at her. He'd known all the wolf packs at one time. But there was nothing to indicate what pack she was from. And he was certain they'd never met before. She narrowed her eyes at him as he examined her.

"My apologies, I didn't mean to frighten you." He held his palms open to show her he meant no harm.

She scoffed and pulled back her arrow until the bowstring was taut. "Do I look stupid? What. Do. You. Want?" She bit out each word.

Her gaze didn't even flicker from his face. She was doggedly persistent about keeping that weapon pointed at him.

She was brave, he had to give her that. "I think I'm the one who should be asking that question."

"Do you work for Akio?"

He hated being lumped in with Akio's lackeys. Working for Akio had never been a choice. But he had to do it to protect Rin. Not that he was going to tell this okami. Shin exposed his canines as he grinned. "I think the better question is: who do you work for?"

"I don't have to tell you anything," she snapped. She talked big, but her hands were shaking.

They weren't going to get anywhere at this rate. One wrong move and she was going to stick him with that arrow. But not if he disarmed her.

He lunged toward her.

She loosed the arrow, but it landed ineffectually in the mud. When he came toward her, she couldn't respond fast enough, encumbered by the bow.

Shin grabbed her around the middle, prepared to throw her over his shoulder. She swung with her bow, clipping him on the jaw and sending him back a few steps.

He recovered quickly, however, and wrenched the bow from her hand. She tried to throw a punch; he dodged it. But she kicked him hard in the gut. It knocked the wind out of him, and she was preparing to hit him over the head when he thrust forward and sent her stumbling backward and onto her rear.

Shin pinned her arms down before she got the chance to swing at him. She was a capable fighter. If she hadn't slipped, she might have gotten the better of him.

Her straw hat had fallen off in the struggle, and he could see her more clearly now. She had a narrow face, brown eyes, and long pointed ears like himself. Her cheeks were flushed from fighting, and her gaze was fierce—

"You bastard, let me go." She kicked and squirmed, cursing him, but pinned as she was it was futile. After a few moments, she exhausted herself and lay heaving beneath him. It wasn't the most ideal position for gaining her trust, but she was the trespasser here, not him. She did not transform. If she did, she would've easily escaped. Curious. Was this all an act perhaps?

"Just tell me: do you work for the dragon?"

"Let me go and I'll tell you," she snarled and bared her canines.

He'd have to take her word for it. He let go of her wrists, and as soon as he did, she pushed forward, planting her palms on his chest. It threw him off balance just long enough for her to slide out from beneath him.

She scrambled for her bow, before racing deeper into the forest.

"Hey!" he shouted after her.

Which she ignored. If one of Akio's lackeys caught her, they wouldn't hesitate to bring her to Akio. He chased after her, grabbing her ankles to bring her back down to the ground. But her legs were too slick with mud and she slipped out of his hands, grabbed her discarded bow, and ran up the hill away from him.

He should let her go. Even if she did work for the dragon. It made no difference. The dragon was weakened by centuries of imprisonment. He wasn't strong enough to break Akio's hold on him. Hoping for an escape was useless. It had been Shin's choice to make this sacrifice. There was no turning back. On the other hand, if Akio found her, he'd torture her. Shin couldn't stand another innocent falling prey to Akio's cruelty.

He raced after her up the hill. By the time he reached the rise, she was nowhere in sight. He scanned the forest trees pegged in the space on both sides, but there was nowhere she could have gone—it was a dead end against a boulder with a flat face.

"You don't need to hide from me," he called out, scenting the air, but the wind was blowing in the wrong direction. "We got off on the wrong foot. I'm not your enemy."

Shin turned in a slow circle, expecting her to be crouched down or backed into a corner like a wounded animal.

From the corner of his eye, something flashed. As he moved to intercept her, something hard collided with the back of his skull.

TWO

Akane looked down at the incapacitated idiot and tossed the rock she'd used to knock him out aside. *Did he really think I was going to fall for that?* She rolled her eyes. He looked like a rag doll, his limbs cast aside carelessly. If he was here, then there were likely others prowling these woods. That would make getting closer to Akio's palace that much harder. It would be safer to retreat, but the head priestess was counting on her.

Akane took a few steps, then pivoted on her heel and went back to his incapacitated body. She couldn't leave a job half done. She should tie him up, just in case he woke up. He stank of boar and wore a collar around his neck. The moment she let her guard down, he'd take her to his master. She dragged him over to a nearby tree. When she got close, she could scent the wolf on him, pungent and earthy. She hated to admit it, but she liked that smell.

Just tie him up, you've wasted enough time as it is. This was supposed to be an information gathering mission. She hadn't planned on running into any of the forest guardian's men. Best to deal with this unexpected complication quickly.

She wound the rope around his chest and bound his arms behind a tree trunk, pulling the knots extra tight, perhaps a bit out of spite. She dusted off her palms and admired her handiwork. *Maybe I should have tied his hands to his feet and then to the tree?* She looked him up and down as she debated. *You're wasting time.* A voice nagged at the back of her mind. She was supposed to get in and out—find out where Akio is taking the priestesses and then report back to the head priestess. This would have to be a sufficient enough job.

She fled, with one last glance back at him. There were bound to be others nearby, and they'd find him. Her quiver strap had torn while she'd wrestled, and now it slammed into her back over and over, the arrows clattering together. It made being stealthy impossible. She should abandon it in favor of stealth, but it had belonged to Mei and she couldn't bear to leave it behind.

Thick fog blanketed the ground and as she ran through it, it did not dissipate. Instead, it reached for her, rising up from her ankles to her waist. Every step she took echoed around her, amplified by the fog.

Something snapped nearby, and she swiveled her head only to realize it was the clattering of her quiver.

Get it together. She shook herself. The okami couldn't have broken free already, could he? She stopped and scanned the forest around her. Her hands gripped hard onto her bow. Very slowly, she removed an arrow from her quiver and notched it.

A small blur of orange darted out from within the fog.

She drew back and was about to fire when a fox froze in front of her. It stared back at her with golden eyes. It was just a mundane fox, no spiritual energy emanated from it.

She lowered her bow and the fox skittered away. *I'm being too jumpy.* She used to hate her heightened hearing and sense of smell; it made the priestesses at the temple nervous when she heard things from far away. But for once she was grateful. If it hadn't been for her abilities, that idiot would have caught her unawares. *Stay on task.*

The fog was getting thicker, and the sound of every step echoed back at her. The hairs on the back of her neck stood on end. She tightened her grip on the bow.

An arm snaked around her neck.

"That was a cruel trick leaving me tied up like that," the wolf whispered in her ear.

She slammed her elbow back into his solar plexus. The idiot doubled over, gasping for breath.

Akane spun to face him, arrow drawn and pointed at him. "How did you break free?" she gasped, her voice shaking despite her best effort to keep it steady. Her mind was racing as she tried to think of how to escape. She could try wrestling him again, but he might just overpower her. Maybe head-butt him and make a run for it, but he might catch up with her.

He chuckled. "Did you really think mundane rope would hold me? Do you know nothing of your own kind?"

Her own kind. They were nothing alike. She served the light, while he was a servant of that vile monster who was kidnapping innocent girls from all over Akatsuki. She shifted from foot to foot.

"I'm not like you," she ground out as she looked around the fog for some weapon or distraction she could use to her advantage.

"Just tell me, do you work for the dragon?"

"I would never serve a monster."

"Huh." He quirked a brow.

"What do you want from me?" She couldn't hide the trembling edge to her words.

"What is an okami in priestess clothing doing in here?" She wasn't sure if the question was meant for her or if he was just musing to himself.

Yokai in the area had been more active than anywhere else. Villages around the region were being terrorized, food stores raided, travelers murdered, and worst of all, they were stealing priestesses from the temples. Surely the wolf knew - maybe he even helped spread the mayhem. He was toying with her, she was certain of it.

"I got lost, so why don't you let me go?"

He tilted his head. "Do I look like an idiot? Last time I let you go you hit me over the head with a rock."

"You were chasing me."

"But why not transform? You could easily escape me if you did."

Of all the things he could have asked her, why that? "And lose my ability to reason?" She smirked. "I think not."

"You're very strange."

"I've answered your questions, now let me go."

"Only if you promise not to hit me again."

Maybe he was stupid. It had to be a trick. But it was her only chance of getting away. The second he let her go, she'd run.

"Alright."

He let go of her wrist first. As soon as it was free, she spun, prepared to strike at him. He dodged it and pulled her quiver from her back. She lunged for it but came up short as he leaped back and out of her reach.

"You said you were going to let me go," she growled.

Quiver in his arms, he leaped onto a low-hanging branch of a tree. He dangled his prize, and she jumped to grab it. Anytime she got close he yanked it away, laughing as he jumped to the next branch.

"This is to make sure I don't end up with an arrow in my back."

She should cut her losses and run away now. The head priestess was counting on her to complete this mission. But she couldn't leave Mei's quiver with this idiot. It would disrespect her memory.

"Go on, leave the forest. If you run into anyone else, they won't be so generous as to let you escape." He shooed her away with a wave of his hand. While he sat down, legs crossed, and laid her quiver over his lap.

Her eyes flickered toward the arrows and then went to his face. "I'm not leaving without my quiver."

"Why would an okami need a bow and arrow when you have perfectly good teeth and claws?" He tilted his head to the side.

She didn't owe him any explanation. "Are you always this infuriating?"

"Most women find me charming, actually."

She scoffed, but her gaze was fixed on her quiver. The leather was embossed with swirling patterns, and when it had been Mei's it was imbued with her spiritual energy. Little of it remained, but it was all Akane had left of her.

"Why don't you come and get it? Or are you afraid of a big bad wolf?" He dangled it down where she could grab it once more.

The wolf inside her stirred. Awakened by some primal urge deep within her. She bared her teeth at him, which were already starting to elongate. If she didn't get away soon, the wolf would take over and then she'd really be in trouble. She couldn't lose control now, not in the middle of enemy territory. Akane took a long breath, soothing the beast inside for now. Chasing him was futile. But it was clear he was arrogant, maybe if she pretended to give up...

"I'm not afraid of a pompous idiot. Know what? Keep them. You're right, I don't need them." She turned her back on him and headed back into the forest. All the while praying her ploy would work.

"You're something of a puzzle," he called after her.

She ignored him and kept walking.

He dropped down in front of her and threw the quiver at her feet.

"Take my advice and leave this place while you still can." He strode away, his arms folded behind his neck.

Akane stared down at the bow and arrow on the ground. She should shoot him in the back just to be certain. But he walked away, disappearing into the mist. She wouldn't take his advice; she still had a mission to complete. It was that fool wolf's mistake to let her go.

A shadow moved through the mist around her. Akane drew her bow once more, pointing it into the opaque fog.

"You said you were letting me go," she snarled, and her canines elongated. She was losing control of her inner wolf. *Not now.* The timing couldn't be worse.

From out of the mist came three boar yokai, their jeering faces twisted into smiles revealing yellowing tusks. Their bodies were covered in coarse black hair, and their feet ended in hooves. They fanned out as they approached her.

"Let you go? You've only just arrived," said the boar yokai on her right.

"Why don't you play with us, girly?" asked the one on her left.

Akane fired three arrows in rapid succession, before turning to run. She hadn't gotten more than a few feet before two monkey yokai dropped out of the treetops, blocking her path.

"You're not going anywhere," said the yokai, "Akio will want to meet you."

THREE

He hadn't gone more than a few feet when laughter broke out behind him. *Shit, that sounded like Akio's lackeys.* He should have escorted her out of the forest. Turning back around, he raced in the direction he'd last seen her. It was just his luck that a group of them were lurking in the forest today.

When he found them, they had surrounded the okami and were taking turns pushing her as she rushed them. Enemies pressed in on all sides, and she couldn't use her bow and arrow. They used her disadvantage to toy with her, opening gaps in their ranks only to close up and knock her backward. She fell to the ground and glared at them. Her eyes were glowing red and her fangs had descended.

A strange power rolled off her in waves. She must have been holding back before. Even he had underestimated her at first. He'd assumed she resisted her wolf form because it was weak. The average okami didn't have much spiritual pressure. But beneath her exterior lay a powerful wolf: one the likes of which he hadn't seen in centuries. Who was this strange okami? Shin hung back another moment, waiting for her to transform and tear them all to shreds. It wouldn't be any great loss - these fools weren't like him. They'd chosen to follow Akio. They might not be as devious as Akio, but they were just as cruel.

Instead of standing up to defend herself, she remained on all fours, her body trembling.

"Tired of playing, wolf?" taunted a boar with a snort.

They were too dense to feel the power unfurling from her. The immensity of her power brushed against his, pushing against his. It was a familiar sensation. One he hadn't realized how much he missed. It had been centuries since he'd seen his own kind. She couldn't be a member of his pack, they'd been dead for a long time now. If only he could see her wolf form, then he might ascertain where she came from.

The yokai closed in as she leaped up, drawing a hidden dagger and swinging at them. The power he had sensed evaporated, not a trace remaining, as if he'd imagined it.

The yokai were not impressed by her display and only laughed in response. They pushed her around a few more times, taking her dagger from her and sending her once more sprawling onto the ground. Shin leaned forward. Was she toying with them? What was her game?

The boar yokai, Riju, pinned her arm behind her back. They'd take her to Akio and she'd face his wrath. He hated trespassers on his land. He'd tried to warn her, and she'd knocked him unconscious and called him Akio's dog. This was her own fault, he supposed. Though he would like to know why she hadn't transformed. He turned to walk away.

"Not giving up? You've got fire," a monkey yokai, Genji hollered with delight.

Shin glanced over his shoulder. There was dried blood on her forehead from a wound that had already closed. Her eyes weren't red like before, but there was fire in them all the same. It was the sort of spark that Akio would love to extinguish. Rin had a similar fire in her. That's why he'd given himself over to Akio all those centuries ago. *I must be the biggest fool.*

"What is this we have here?" Shin asked as he stepped out of the shadows and into the clearing.

The yokai all turned to him as he arrived, including the okami who was glaring at him as if he'd been the one torturing her. He pretended not to notice and gave the yokai a deadly smile. He might be Akio's dog, but he wasn't a tamed dog.

When he'd first arrived in Akio's palace, a group of Akio's lackeys had thought to humiliate him by beating him within an inch of his life. What they hadn't expected was for him to destroy them before they'd gotten the chance. He had been half mad in those days. He hadn't cared if he lived or died.

Shin had lost it all. The woman he loved, his freedom, and his best friend. He'd hoped Akio would kill him to punish him for it but keeping him alive inflicted much more pain. No matter how many lackeys Shin killed, Akio wouldn't grant him freedom in death. As time passed, he'd grown numb to it all, but his reputation as a killer had been made.

As he approached the monkey yokai hopped backward, landing on nearby tree branches, their long tails swaying back and forth. Their faces were a cross between human and ape. Their large ears turned red and their beady brown eyes were trained on Shin. They'd retreated both to put distance between them and Shin and give them the higher ground in case he turned on them. The boar, Riju, who was holding the okami, wrinkled his pig nose and furrowed bushy brows. His companions stood one step behind them, hands resting on the hilt of their swords.

"We found her wandering the woods," said Riju with a snort. He stared at Shin, emboldened by his role as leader of their gang.

Shin looked over at the she-wolf lazily as if they'd never met before. Her pupils were pinpricks at the center of glowing red eyes. Given the chance, she'd tear out his throat - he was certain of it.

"Is this how we handle trespassers now?" Shin asked in a bored tone while he examined his nails.

The yokai shared looks. They were smart enough to know a trap when they saw one.

"We were just having some fun," said Genji in a screeching tone.

"And if you'd killed her before Akio questioned her, then what?"

None of them would look at him.

"If you'd all rather play games, then I'll take the girl to Akio myself." Riju let her go and she fell forward into a crouch. Her plans were written all over her face. He gave the briefest shake of his head, hoping she'd realize he was trying to help her before she attacked.

She let him approach, though her gaze was wary. He grabbed her by the forearm, pulling her to her feet, and leaned in. "Just play along," he whispered.

She took a swing at his head, which he easily dodged. After a brief staged tussle, he twisted her arm behind her back and marched her forward.

"You're just going to take credit for this find?" asked Riju.

"I found her first, but she slipped me. Thanks for catching her." He tipped his head in thanks.

"Well. That is…"

"Do me a favor and don't tell Akio I almost let her go." He grinned, baring his teeth in warning. Before they could question him, he pulled on Akane's arm, leading her away. The key to any kind of deception was acting confident. If he kept walking, none of them would stop him. He kept his head cocked slightly, listening to make sure they weren't followed.

The yokai grumbled but departed, and Shin pulled the okami in the direction of Akio's palace. Only once he was certain no one was watching did he let her go.

She spun to face him, her hands up in defense once more.

"Why did you do that?" she asked. Her eyes were no longer red, but there was still a strange feral quality to her posture. Her hands were clenched tight, and her eyes darted all around like a wolf cornered.

"I think the words you're looking for are thank you."

She took a step back.

Shin shook his head and laughed. "Come with me, if you want to get out of these woods alive."

She hesitated a moment, as if she was debating whether or not she wanted to trust him. Her hair had come loose from her braid and caressed her face in loose strands. There was something charming about her scowls. Not since Rin had he met another okami nearly as stubborn.

Thinking about Rin brought back a flood of painful memories. It awakened an aching loneliness that still lingered at the darkest corners of his heart. He needed to get the okami out of here before he started having even crazier ideas. He started walking. If she decided not to follow him, that was her problem. He'd already taken a risk helping her escape. He wasn't going to kill himself over a fool.

She followed after him, and he led her to the edge of the forest, taking twisting pathways down rarely used animal trails that he'd discovered over centuries prowling these woods. They kept a wide berth of the typical patrol outposts, until they arrived at the edge of the forest where it abutted the human farmlands. He waved his arm in the direction of the rice paddies.

"Thanks," she muttered under her breath.

"Sorry, I didn't catch that."

She looked up at him, meeting his gaze for the first time. Without meaning to he found himself comparing her to Rin: the sweep of her lips, turned down in a scowl were nothing like Rin's mischievous grin. Her thick brown hair was dull compared to Rin's auburn waves. Perhaps he'd saved her out of lingering feelings for Rin. But this woman was nothing compared to her, just a stubborn okami who'd wandered where she shouldn't have.

"Forget it," she said before bolting.

She was a red and white blur moving over the rice paddies before disappearing over the horizon.

He leaned forward as he watched her, the only thing keeping him from crossing the perimeter of Akio's domain was the heavy metal collar around his neck. He grabbed it, tugging on it. There was no use trying to take it off. It would never budge. Akio owned him, body and soul. There was no use wishing for things that he couldn't have.

Shin transformed into his wolf form and then he ran through the forest, his feet flying. Dappled sunlight filtered through the green canopy of the trees. His paws skimmed the top of a bush as he leaped, and when he landed the dead leaves danced on the air, caught up in the wind he'd created.

A rabbit nibbled on new grass, its back to him. The flicker of its white tail caught his attention, and he slowed to study it. His muscles tensed, poised to lunge. All his animal instincts were telling him to kill. It had been too long since he'd let the wolf out and after today he needed the release.

There'd be no pain. He was downwind, so the kill would be quick and clean. It would sate the wolf's bloodlust for a time. And yet he hesitated. His inner wolf was not his master. Akio would likely find out about the okami. And when he did, he'd be furious. But what could Akio do to him? He wouldn't kill him, he needed Shin. His hatred of the dragon would outweigh his anger at Shin's betrayal. And it's not as if it would come at a surprise. Akio knew Shin wasn't loyal to him. No matter how Akio tried to force Shin to be his pawn, Shin would always be loyal to the dragon.

To add insult to injury, if Shin were summoned reeking of blood, it would make Akio even angrier. Akio hated anything that lacked refinement. According to Akio, hunting was for heathens, not his pets.

The wind changed direction. The rabbit lifted its head as it caught his scent. It bolted for cover. Shin smelled it too. The bitter scent of metal. Then like an invisible hand tapping on his shoulder, spiritual energy brushed against him. A warning and an announcement.

"Can I help you?" Shin asked, his gaze fixed on where the rabbit had escaped. If only he could follow it.

The man stepped out of the shadows. He wore a billowing black haori and hakama, a black mask which covered the lower half of his face, and an ax strapped to his back. His long black hair was tied in a topknot.

"You've been summoned," said the huntsman, his voice muffled by the mask.

The dark figure had always made the hairs on the back of his neck stand on end. Akio had likely sent him because he was the only person Shin truly feared. All Shin knew about the yokai was that he was ancient and powerful, but no one knew where Akio had found him or anything about his past at all. The lesser yokai stayed clear of Shin, but everyone feared the huntsman - Akio's ruthless killer. He was likely one of the First Children, and a replacement for his old servant, Naoki, who'd left Akio's service centuries ago. If only Shin could be so lucky as to escape.

"What for this time?" Shin asked, his tone light and still hoping Akio hadn't found out.

"That is for the guardian to tell you."

That wasn't a good sign.

Akio's palace was at the center of the forest. It burst from the treetops, with sloped dark roofs that stood out against the white-washed walls. The buildings sprawling across the compound were encircled by a deep canyon. The only entrance into the palace was over a narrow rope bridge. Above it all, a massive tree with bright white blossoms scattered white petals, which danced on the wind and littered the stone courtyard. The tree was the source of Akio's power and marked him as guardian of the forest.

The tension in the air thickened. The guards, a pair of oni, were massive beasts with thick gray hides and two eyes between the pair of them. Unlike most oni, Akio forced them to wear bright red armor over their navy hakama and haori. They were particularly rigid today.

"How mad is he?" Shin asked them.

"Furious," grunted Sotaru, on the left.

"What did you do now?" asked Renzo on the right.

Shin shrugged. He wasn't going to give himself away that easily. Inside, his hide was twitching, anticipating a beating that was surely headed his way. He made his way down the twisting hallways of the palace. The passageways were ever-changing, and if you didn't know your way around, you'd get lost within the labyrinth. The palace itself was alive, fueled by Akio's guardian power and the tree. Shin had heard rumors that Akio made a deal with the ancient tree spirit, who'd given him the power to become forest guardian.

When Shin approached Akio's throne room, he could hear his roars. It shook the ceiling. The guards at the door opened up and Shin slunk in casually. Akio tossed a pitcher of sake against the wall, and it shattered into pieces. Alcohol sprayed Shin's face and clothes. He wiped it with the back of his hand, flicking it onto the floor.

Akio, a boar yokai, was much larger than his subjects. He was twice Shin's size, both wide and tall, and was covered in coarse wiry black hair. Though he looked like an over-sized wild boar, he wore a fine silk haori and hakama in the fashion of the human realm and wore a courtier's hat on top of his head. Though he tried to mimic human form, he could not get rid of the hooves or his boar-like face.

"How dare he!" Akio growled, and then seeing him, pointed at Shin with a hoof. "You!"

"Me," Shin replied blandly, pointing at his own chest. Normally he wouldn't have played with fire this way, but he wanted to get this over with quickly.

Akio stood up to his full height. He filled the space, blocking out the light from the room's brazier and casting Shin into shadow, his eyes glowing red from rage.

"Did you think I wouldn't find out?" He sprayed spittle onto Shin's face.

Shin wiped the spit away and avoided making eye contact. "I was hoping you wouldn't."

Akio trembled, his face turned ruddy. "Who was she, the dragon's spy? Have you been feeding him information about me?"

"I haven't spoken to the dragon, other than what you've ordered me to say. I belong to you, master." Shin bowed his head, the words bitter in his mouth. The only way to appease Akio was to play to his ego.

Akio's hoof hung in the air. Shin waited for the blow to fall, but it never did. Instead, Akio stomped back over to his enormous cushion and sat. The platters of food and drink tipped over. Dumplings and rice were scattered across the floor, while even more sake stained the tatami. Akio called for his sake, with a jerk of his hoof. A servant rushed forward with a fresh jug. Akio drank deeply, spilling the milky liquid down his throat and wetting the front of his haori. When he was finished he smacked his lips. The color had gone from his face and he was almost smiling, which was more concerning than his anger.

"That's right, you belong to me." He smiled, and it made Shin's intestines squirm. "I am willing to forgive your transgression. Clean that up." He pointed at the shattered pottery.

Shin's head shot up. He knew what was coming next. He could try and fight it, but it only made the punishment that much worse. He walked over and squatted down, picking up pieces, stacking them on one another.

"Not like that," Akio said. "Use your mouth."

Shin clenched his empty hand. Even he had his limits. He had to have some pride left to him.

"Now," Akio commanded.

The word was laced with power. He could not disobey. His collar tightened, choking him, and a part of him would rather die than stoop so low. His damn body struggled for air and he transformed into his true wolf form. Then one by one, he picked up the broken fragments, the sharp edges cut his tongue and filled his mouth with blood.

He spit them out onto a cloth, provided by a servant. Blood dripped from his mouth, and onto the floor, mixing with saliva and staining his muzzle.

"And the rest," Akio said.

Shin looked at him, considering trying to tear his throat out. He wouldn't succeed, but at least he'd have the satisfaction of rebellion.

"Do it," Akio urged. Fiery pain rippled outward from his collar, igniting all his nerves at once. He stood his ground, his body convulsing until the pain subsided. When it was over, Shin's tail hung between his legs. Rebellion was pointless. Akio always got what he wanted. He lapped up the sickening mixture of his blood and spilled sake.

"Very good. But I don't think you've learned your lesson." The soft croon of his voice sent a chill down his spine.

"Bring the girl back by the next full moon or I will lock you away for a hundred years in the dungeon."

Shin shuddered at the thought. The dungeon was the cruelest punishment Akio could devise. The cells were completely devoid of light. Not only pitch black but it suppressed all spiritual power. Spending one night in that cell had made him feel like he could lose his mind. A hundred years was worse than a death sentence.

He knew it had been a mistake in helping her. He'd been a fool to even try and disobey Akio.

"Yes, Master." Shin bowed.

Four

A group of priestesses was clustered together whispering when Akane's charge, Tomoe, passed by on the way to Tomoe's morning prayers.

"We have to go, look!" Hitome, one of the girls, exclaimed.

Tomoe's head snapped in their direction.

Akane, already sensing her excitement, tried to intervene by putting herself between Tomoe and the girls. "We don't—"

Tomoe had that gleam in her eye. It was too late now. Tomoe was always of a singular mind, and she couldn't resist gossiping with the other girls. Tomoe veered from their normal route and ran over to the girls.

Akane chased after her. "There's no time for this—"

"What did I miss?" Tomoe asked the other girls.

The girls looked nervously to Akane, who scowled at them over Tomoe's shoulder. Usually their fear bothered her, but today it was in her favor. If they were too afraid to speak in front of her, maybe Tomoe would lose interest, and then they could get back on track. This temple had been built in service to the kami. Every generation a girl was chosen to become the living host for the kami. Tomoe was this generation's host and it was Akane's job as shrine guardian to make sure she remained pure. The gossiping was bad enough. But if she missed her daily purification rituals of prayer at morning, noon, and night, impurity could taint her soul and she'd be rejected by the kami. Which meant death. Akane couldn't let that happen again.

"Tomoe," Akane said sternly.

"Please. It will just be a minute." Tomoe widened her large, soulful eyes that Akane could never say no to.

Akane sighed. "Just a minute."

Tomoe blessed her with a dazzling smile. That was how she got away with so much - she was charming and easy to love. Unlike Akane, whose nature and temper terrified the priestesses. They were right to fear her. Just beneath the surface was a monster biding its time and preparing to attack. She'd gotten close to losing control in the forest. And what if she had? Would she have ever come to her senses again?

"Don't leave me in suspense. Did Haruhi get caught sneaking out to meet her lover? Or did Osami get scolded again for sleeping during prayer?" Tomoe asked, leaning closer, peering around them dramatically.

The girls whispered, struggling as they all tried to hide behind one another, until they pushed one girl forward as their chosen representative. She chewed her lip as she looked at Akane through her lashes.

"Get it over with," Akane said with a heavy sigh and a wave of her hand.

The girl addressed the ground. "A woman is at the gate asking to be taken in as an apprentice."

This wasn't anything too unusual. Girls arrived at the temple all the time. Most often the head priestess turned them away. On the rare occasion one was suited to become an acolyte, it took years of service before she could become a fully-fledged priestess. It was nothing to get excited over.

"Then go and notify the head priestess, instead of gossiping." Then steering Tomoe by the shoulders, she tried to direct her away from them. They'd wasted enough time already.

"She's already been notified, but I heard the girl wasn't human," one of the girls said from the back of the group.

Akane's grip loosened on Tomoe's shoulders. She turned to the priestesses with a furrowed brow.

"That's not something to joke about," Akane snapped.

"It's true," the priestess said in a trembling voice.

In the blink of an eye, Tomoe was running for temple entrance.

Akane shouted her name to no avail. There was no deterring Tomoe once something had caught her attention. Akane's chest tightened. Had she been followed? She hadn't noticed anyone. Whoever they were, Akane had to protect the temple.

A small flood of priestesses and acolytes streamed toward the gate, joining a crowd gathered there. They chattered amongst themselves, making no attempts to hide their curiosity.

Tomoe weaved through them with ease, making her way to the front of the crowd. Akane followed and the girls moved out of her way, avoiding eye contact.

Over the sea of girls was the snowy white head of the head priestess. The new girl she was speaking with looked normal—dark hair, plain face, dressed like a peasant.

Until she tucked a stray lock behind her ear—her pointed ear.

Then they hadn't been exaggerating. She was a yokai.

What was this yokai doing here? Why would she walk up here and dare ask for entrance? The girl was beautiful, in a fierce sort of way. With long limbs, an angular face, and wild dark hair that could not be tamed by her ponytail, there was something familiar about her that Akane couldn't quite put her finger on. She had a sword, perhaps an enchanted blade judging from its bitter smell, and the girl herself stank of wolf. Apart from the okami Akane had seen in the guardian's woods, she hadn't seen a wolf in ages.

The girl's scent was almost familiar, but Akane had never met this monster before. Had she? Maybe that okami she'd met had her followed.

The head priestess would never let a yokai into the temple. And if this yokai tried, the head priestess could turn her to ash with her song. The barriers would protect the temple from intruders. Ever since priestesses had started going missing they'd strengthened their defenses, adding charms and incantations to their entire perimeter. No one with ill intentions could enter these sacred grounds. And if it came down to it, Akane was charged with protecting the temple from attack.

The head priestess turned away from the okami, presumably after telling her to leave and not return. She couldn't hear over the chatter of the assembled priestesses. As the old woman hobbled away, however, the okami didn't turn and leave. She took a step toward the barrier.

The air shimmered, like ripples in a pond. The barrier had always protected the temple, it would keep her back.

Energy sparked against the intruder's flesh, then faded as she stepped through. This yokai had just crossed the barrier.

She wasn't sure how the okami had gotten through, but she didn't have time to ask questions. It was her duty to protect the temple. Akane launched herself at the yokai, swinging for her face, landing a punch.

The yokai girl staggered back.

Behind Akane, the acolytes screamed and scattered to escape the fight.

The yokai wiped blood from her lip before giving Akane an arrogant smile.

Akane circled her. The yokai girl was perhaps a head taller, but Akane's speed and the element of surprise was on her side with her first blow. Landing a second would be harder.

The girl smiled, and it sent a shiver down her spine. She just had to keep this yokai busy long enough for the priestess to sing and immobilize her.

The yokai struck to the right, and Akane fumbled.

A feint. The yokai came around behind her, tapping her on the rear-end with her palm.

Akane spun, swinging at her, but missing by an inch. Her canines had descended, but she didn't care. She was out for blood.

"My, what big teeth you have," the girl taunted as she leaped out of Akane's reach once more.

The last thread reining in her temper snapped. She barreled into the yokai girl, catching her around the middle and slamming her back against the wall.

The wolf inside her was howling, held back by the merest strength of will. If the okami pushed Akane further, Akane would lose control completely, and the entire temple would be in danger.

The taller woman was pinned against the wall with Akane's hand around her throat, and still she smirked. Akane pressed down harder on her throat.

"What do you think you're doing?" the head priestess shouted and hobbled toward them.

Akane turned her head toward the priestess. The girl swept out her leg, knocking Akane's feet from beneath her. She landed hard on her back.

The girl drew her blade and pressed it against Akane's throat. She scowled up at her.

"You almost had me there." The girl panted for breath.

The head priestess approached the pair of them, and the yokai removed the sword from Akane's throat and took a step back, bowing reverently to the head priestess.

"What were you thinking?" the head priestess asked, her white brows pulled together as she stared down at Akane.

Akane jumped to her feet and pointed at the yokai. "She was about to attack you when you turned your back!"

"She was going to do no such thing. She is a temple guardian like yourself."

"She doesn't look like a shrine guardian." Akane threw out her arms, pointing at the yokai to make her point.

Akane glared at the girl who smiled mischievously back. She'd met plenty of temple guardians in her time. They were the chosen of the divine. All of the others she'd met were refined - they seemed to glow with the blessing of the kami. This yokai was different, there was a wild energy to her that made her uneasy. Besides she couldn't shake this feeling they'd met somewhere before though she couldn't say where.

"I think I can tell the difference between a wild yokai and a temple guardian, don't you?" the head priestess replied.

Akane lowered her head. Under normal circumstances, she would concede to the head priestess' wisdom. She was a powerful priestess, and she'd never intentionally put the temple at risk. But it couldn't be a coincidence that after escaping the guardian's okami, Akane would run into another.

The head priestess came closer to Akane and put her hand on top of her bowed head. "This poor child has lost her temple to a yokai attack. The least we can do is give her a place to stay, hmm?"

"Yes, Head Priestess," Akane said.

She glared at the girl behind the head priestess who gave her a lazy smile. Akane turned away from her, lips curled in disgust.

The head priestess studied Akane and then the girl. "I think this will be a good opportunity for you. Akane, we are in need of another temple guardian."

Akane's head shot up. "How can we entrust the safety of the temple to a stranger?"

"A good point. You shall test her to make sure she's worthy."

"But—"

"Are you questioning the will of the kami?" the head priestess asked, invoking her role as speaker for the goddess.

Akane lowered her head once more. The head priestess hobbled past her and started toward the palace buildings. The acolytes had started to disperse as well.

"You cannot be everywhere at once, Akane," the head priestess said. "Having a second pair of eyes could be a blessing in these difficult times."

She balled her hands into fists at her side. They did need the help with yokai attacking shrines, and Akane couldn't protect them all. But she didn't trust this okami.

"You fight pretty well," the yokai said, with that damn arrogant smile still on her face.

Akane ground her teeth. She could have beaten her. She never should have taken her eyes off the girl for a second.

"Thanks." Akane turned to march away.

"Aren't you going to tell me your name at least?" the girl called after her.

She considered ignoring her, but if it got back to the head priestess, she'd scold her. Akane had already disappointed the head priestess enough lately. "Akane," she said through gritted teeth.

Akane kept on walking and the okami called after her again. "You're not going to ask me what my name is?"

Akane took a deep breath and turned to the okami with a forced smile. "And what's your name?"

The girl looked her up and down, rubbing her chin as she studied her. Akane had to resist the urge to grind her teeth to dust.

"It's Shinon," she said at last.

"Welcome to the temple, Shinon." Akane turned and marched away. *I'm going to find out why you're here, so don't get comfortable.*

FIVE

Soft snores filled the air as Shin lay on his futon. The shrine maidens were fascinated by him it seemed and had pestered him relentlessly with questions when he'd been assigned a place to sleep. The head priestess had to scold them and tell them to sleep before he'd been free of them. Pretending to sleep was just an additional precaution.

Soft footsteps crossed the dormitory. One of the acolytes, probably. He squeezed his eyes shut just in case. The footsteps moved closer and the scent of wolf wafted toward him.

He leaped out of bed, nearly head-butting Akane standing over his futon. They stared at each other, each poised for a fight.

Shin lowered his arms to his side and smiled. "To what do I owe the pleasure?"

She glared back, unamused. "It's time to start work," Akane replied flatly.

She was a strange creature, fierce and clearly distrustful of her own kind. He'd met plenty of temple guardians throughout the years. Most were stuck up and self-important, but none of them hated yokai. They were of a kind; the only distinction was who they served. The role of a disposed shrine guardian fit well enough, and it wasn't entirely false. Though Akio was vile, he was worshiped by the local farmers and nobles as a deity, and Shin was his servant.

Shin looked at the dim morning light. "This early?"

"Is that a problem?" Akane asked with a brow rising toward her hairline.

Was this her idea of a challenge? Well, perhaps being agreeable would bring her around. Even if he could capture her, she wouldn't come easily. He needed to gain her trust to lure her back to Akio. But time was of the essence. He'd just got there and already she seemed determined to hate him. He'd hoped a disguise would have helped, but it seemed she was the distrustful type.

"Not at all." He jumped out of bed and followed Akane out into the brisk early morning air. The cold breeze felt good, and he stretched. "What do we have to do exactly?"

"We escort Tomoe through her morning routine."

"Sounds easy enough."

Akane assumed a hurried pace, which Shin matched. Everything was silent. No one had risen from bed yet, and long shadows shrouded everything in darkness. The feeble light was gray and damp. What could he say to cut this chilly silence?

"Have you been a shrine guardian long?"

When they arrived at a door, not much different than all the others, Akane knocked on it. "Tomoe, time to wake up."

There was a loud groan from inside.

"What's inside, an oni?" he teased.

Akane gave him a deadpan stare. "This is the kamigakari in training, I would appreciate it if you didn't insult her in such a way.

Her braid swung as she turned to slide open the door. *She doesn't have much of a sense of humor, does she?* How could he compare her to Rin? They were nothing alike. He was too sentimental for his own good. He should have left her to her fate, then he wouldn't be in this mess.

Instead of a fierce oni inside the room, there was a young girl with tousled black hair rubbing the sleep from her eyes.

"Akane," she whined. "Can't I just sleep in?"

"You know the rules. You have to be up to greet the sun."

"Would it really hurt if she slept in?" Shin asked.

Akane's nostrils flared before she turned her back on him once more and walked over to a nearby dresser. She pulled out the girl's red hakama and white haori. Shin, not wanting to invade her privacy, turned away while Akane dressed her.

Once she was dressed, they headed out. The temple was rather small, containing two dormitories with sloped roofs. One dormitory housed the acolytes and the other housed the priestesses. A separate building housed the head priestess, her second-in-command, and Tomoe, the kamigakari in training. And finally, there was a dining hall where everyone ate together and this is where they stopped first.

The room was crowded with priestesses in red and white, and acolytes in brown, all sitting according to their rank. The low tables were laden with plates of food. At the far end of the room was a separate table for the head priestess and other leaders of the shrine. Tomoe took her seat at this table, while Shin and Akane fell in place behind her.

"When do we eat?" Shin asked Akane, hoping to tease out a smile. Yokai did not need to eat as often as humans. It was a much more recreational pastime for their kind.

Akane did not even so much as flick her gaze toward him.

After Tomoe finished her meal, they headed to the shrine building. Compared to the plain, brown buildings in the rest of the temple, the shrine building was opulent. White-washed walls were accented by red columns and gold medallions. The entrance was guarded by a red torii arch and from it a string of ofuda danced in a light breeze.

The inner shrine was a small, square room, the floor covered in tatami mats. A small altar held a portrait of the kami. She was depicted as a beautiful woman with long black hair, her body illuminated in gold. In one hand she held a branch, and her other hand was open, beckoning to the watcher. Unlike other shrines he'd entered, Shin felt none of the spiritual energy of a kami. It was almost as if this place was dead.

Incense was being burned and the scent tickled at his nose. The heavy scents dulled his senses. Shin crinkled his nose. Tomoe knelt before the portrait of the kami, lighting even more incense as she pressed her hands together in prayer.

Shin rubbed his nose. The incense was driving him crazy.

"How much longer does she have to pray?" Shin asked.

"Shh," Akane warned.

He sighed.

The minutes ticked by painfully slow. Akane kept her head leaned forward, her eyes sparkling as she stared at the portrait of the kami. She was very devout. That surprised him. It was rather refreshing. He'd given up on the kami long ago. Shin had been so busy staring at Akane, he didn't realize the prayers had ended. Akane caught him. He tried smiling at her again, but she turned away.

"You could show some respect for the kami, you are a temple guardian after all." She quirked a brow at him.

"I have nothing but respect for the kami."

She rolled her eyes and looked away.

"Shall we?" Tomoe addressed Akane, keeping her back to Shin.

"What's next?" Shin asked.

Tomoe headed for the exit and Akane followed after her. Being excluded was new and painful. He was a pack animal by nature, and being ignored by another of his kind stung. He would have thought after centuries of loneliness he would get used to it. But it never got easier.

On their way back to the dormitories, they passed by the practice yard. It was tiny in comparison to the one in Akio's palace - large enough only for two combatants at once. It looked like it doubled as a storage yard for grain and garden tools. The only weapons were a few rusty swords lying on the ground. Priestesses sparred in a practice yard with staff and sword. As they passed by, Tomoe slowed to a stop. The longing on her face was unmistakable. Akane placed her hand on the girl's shoulder and with one last, lingering look she kept walking. When Tomoe looked away, her eyes were lifeless.

The remainder of the day was the longest of Shin's life. The pair continued to ignore him, despite multiple attempts. After night prayers, not to be mistaken for morning and afternoon prayers, Akane deposited the girl back in her room. Shin remained outside while Akane dressed her in her night clothes. Human lives were so fleeting, it seemed a shame to waste it with ritual and prayer. Even the kami didn't spend this much time in prayer. How had the girl not been driven mad by the tedium of it all?

He leaned against the wall as Akane came out and shut the door. "Did I pass?" he asked her.

With her face to the door, she took a long breath, then shot him a dirty look. "Hardly. I just wanted to see if the holy prayers would burn you."

Shin smirked. It would take more than one girl's half-hearted prayers to hurt him. But he wasn't going to tell her that.

"There's always tomorrow."

She scoffed. Then with a quick pivot of her foot, she strode down the hall. She wasn't going to make this easy, was she?

As he was on his way to the dormitories, something darted by, just at the edge of his periphery. He tilted his head to the side. The human eye wouldn't have noticed the figure crouched in the shadows. The girl, Tomoe, looked both ways. She'd noticed him lingering and froze in place.

He turned his back to her and whistled to himself as he strolled in the opposite direction. Once he was around the corner of a building, he hid himself and waited. After a few heartbeats, she bolted across an open courtyard and hid in the shadows of another building. After a quick glance, she scurried once more out of sight toward the practice yard. He smiled to himself.

In the practice yard, Tomoe and another girl conferred with furtive glances. The second girl clutched a wooden blade.

"Ready?" Tomoe asked her.

The girl looked around for the hundredth time in a few seconds before nodding slowly.

They took their positions, bowed to each other and then their bout began. Circling one another, their weapons poised, they both hesitated to go on the offensive. It was a lack of confidence in one and stubbornness in the other that held them back. Tomoe lunged forward, while the other girl leaped out of the way.

Shin leaned back against the wall, watching their play, hidden from view. It seemed Tomoe was not the ideal kamigakari she pretended to be.

She lunged again. Her expression was fierce and determined. Like an arrow released from its bowstring, she struck her opponent. The shy girl blocked, but it was sloppy. Her wooden sword slipped and struck Tomoe on her hand.

Tomoe cried out and dropped her sword, waving her injured hand and blowing on her fingers.

"Oh, Tomoe, I'm so sorry. Are you all right? I knew this was a bad idea," the second girl fretted, looking around.

"It's not that bad. I can keep practicing." Tomoe clenched and unclenched her fingers.

"I don't think we should. If the head priestess finds out—"

"I've told you, she won't." Tomoe sounded confident but even from a distance he could see the uncertainty in her gaze.

"But I hurt you! What if it scars and you cannot accept the kami's spirit?"

Tomoe rolled her eyes. "It's fine. I'm better already."

The girl wrung her hands together, looking everywhere but at Tomoe. "But next time—"

"I don't know how you think you're going to hurt me when you refuse to even fight me properly!" Tomoe threw her hands up in exasperation.

"I'm sorry," the girl said to the ground. "I don't think we should do this anymore." She dropped her sword and bolted away.

Tomoe made a half-hearted attempt to chase her before turning and kicking the fallen sword.

"Fine! I don't need you," she shouted after the girl. After picking up the sword, she assumed a fighting stance and swung the blade in a wide sloppy arch.

It was painful to watch. He couldn't just stand by. Shin stepped forward. Tomoe was halfway through some complicated spin when she noticed him. She attempted to hide the sword behind the folds of her hakama.

"What are you doing here?" she asked, scooting away as he came closer.

"I came to practice my swordplay. It helps me sleep." He picked up a wooden blade and tossed it in his hand before doing a series of thrusts and parries against an invisible enemy. Tomoe watched with her mouth hanging open.

"Would you want to practice with me?" he asked her.

She eyed him up and down. "Did Akane send you?"

"No, I don't think she really likes me," he said in a conspiratorial whisper.

Tomoe laughed. "No, not really."

In truth this was the most exciting thing that had happened to him all day. He was certain Akane would be livid if she found out. Consider it revenge for ignoring him all day. But out loud he said, "So how about it, want to spar?"

Her eyes were wide and eager. After one quick glance around, she removed the practice sword from behind her back with a sheepish look.

They took their positions and bowed to one another. Her skill was as he would expect, but she had good reflexes and was quick on her feet. There was no way to fight her and not hold back. If he fought her at his full strength, he would surely hurt her. But he knew she wanted to be challenged, and she was never going to learn if she wasn't.

He kept her on her toes, spinning and running to dodge his attacks. What he hadn't accounted for was her lack of stamina. At first she was doing great; she could dodge most of his attacks, and she landed a few of her own. Sweat dripped down her forehead, and her hair was plastered to her skin.

Shin thrust forward, a strike that should have been easy enough to avoid, but she didn't get out of the way in time and he struck her hard in the gut. Tomoe doubled over and fell to her knees. In an instant, he dropped his sword and rushed to her side.

"I'm so sorry!" he said, putting his arm around her as she heaved for breath. He'd knocked the wind out of her.

"Get away from her!" Akane screamed as she ran toward them. She grabbed Shin by the shoulder, tossing him aside. Shin fell onto his back.

"I'm fine," Tomoe rasped.

"What were you doing?" Akane said as she pulled up Tomoe's haori to reveal a red lump on her stomach. It would be a bruise by the morning. Akane's hands hovered over the injury.

"We were just practicing." Tomoe winced as she tried to readjust.

"What were you even doing out of bed?"

"I just wanted to learn how to sword fight. What if the yokai attack the temple? I should be able to defend myself."

"That's what I'm here for."

"You can't always be here."

Akane rested her hand on the girl's head. It was surprisingly tender. He'd thought her rather cold and unfeeling, but clearly she cared for the girl.

Tomoe pulled away. "I'm not a child anymore, Akane."

"I know that. It's just you cannot do these things. You're to be the kamigakari and it's not appropriate."

"Every moment of the day belongs to the temple. Can't I have a moment just for me?" she asked.

"I know, but this is your destiny."

She jumped to her feet. "I don't care about that. I don't want to be the kamigakari."

"You shouldn't think things like that. Negative thoughts lead to impurities."

Tomoe bit her lip. "What do you care more about the kami or my happiness?"

Akane's face blanched. She opened and closed her mouth. But no words came out. Shin hadn't realized just how devout Akane was. Perhaps that explained her hatred of yokai. The kami considered themselves divine and superior to yokai. Perhaps her loyalty to her kami had convinced her those who did not serve the kami were evil.

Tomoe shook her head. "I knew it." She turned and stomped off, leaving Akane standing in the middle of the practice ground.

This was his chance to comfort her. Shin took a step toward her, but as soon as he did, Akane spun to face him. She jutted a finger in his direction. "This is all your fault!" she growled.

He put his hands up in a defensive pose. "We were just practicing. She'll heal."

Akane came very close, her face inches from his, her fangs had descended and there was the hint of that wild, red glint in her eye. "The head priestess will hear about this."

She spun on her heel and chased after Tomoe. When she was out of sight, Shin exhaled. He'd really messed up this time, hadn't he? *She's never going to trust me. How can I get her back to Akio now?*

Six

As usual, Tomoe had locked herself in her room. Akane slammed her fist against the door. "I know you're angry, but I'm only trying to do what's best for you."

There was no answer. Akane sighed and leaned her head back against the wall.

"It's not that I don't care. It's just, I don't want you to suffer Mei's fate—" Her voice caught on the last word. Tomoe was young and she didn't understand, yet. If the kami rejected her, she would die. There had been so many times she tried to tell her, but she didn't have the heart to scare her. Akane took a deep breath, trying to rid the horrid visions dancing in her head. Memories of that horrible day swam to the surface. Mei had died because the kami had deemed her impure. She refused to let that happen to Tomoe. Akane took a ragged breath to calm herself lest she become overwhelmed by her own thoughts.

"I'm coming in," Akane announced. The only way to keep her demons at bay was to keep moving.

Tomoe sat in the curve of her circular window, staring out at the dark horizon. The moon was full and from their vantage on a hilltop, the Imperial City was visible. The twinkle of firelight from the surrounding city spread out across the landscape like stars in the night sky. In the center of it all, the White Palace was a full moon on a winter's night. White-washed walls enclosed it on all sides, but the sloping roofs of the palace buildings loomed over the walls like dark sentinels.

Over her centuries of service, the palace had gone from a single stronghold to the sprawling, and tangled monolith in the center of Akatsuki. Tomoe had come to the temple when she was a little more than five years old. She'd told Akane she had few memories of the palace, nor did she miss it. But Akane had her doubts.

"I can't do this anymore," Tomoe said, her stubborn stare focused on the horizon.

"And where else would you go? Back there?" Akane gestured toward the palace.

Tomoe scrunched her nose. "No. The palace would be even worse."

They both stood in silence. Akane crossed her arms over her chest. Tomoe was destined to become the kamigakari. More than ever, the temple needed one. It had been nearly fifty years since one had ascended. The kamigakari brought peace to the region, saving the land from drought, famine, and natural disaster. The farms' yields were becoming less and less with each passing year, and recent storms had nearly destroyed half the Imperial City. But how could she convince Tomoe to make such a sacrifice for the greater good?

"Sometimes, I think about just leaving it all behind, pick up my sword and go," Tomoe said.

The very idea sent a wave of panic through Akane. She could see a hundred scenarios in which Tomoe was either raped, killed, or both.

"It's not safe out there," Akane said.

"You think I couldn't defend myself?" she asked, her gaze accusing.

"Even against a yokai?" Akane said.

"If a yokai tried to attack me, I'd just use my ofuda and seal them." She pulled out the long rectangle piece of paper from her sleeve with her free hand.

"It wouldn't take them long before they realized there was no power in that ofuda."

Tomoe crossed her arms over her chest and tilted her head up. There was a blush staining her cheeks.

They often joked about how little spiritual power Tomoe had, the girl destined for the highest honor, but she was worse at incantations and songs that most acolytes knew. It was strange that her spiritual powers had not yet manifested. Tomoe pretended it didn't bother her, but as the years went by, it went from a mere oddity to a real concern. Akane had served many initiates. But never before had she seen one get this close to her time and still be unable to master even the most basic skills.

"I'm sorry," Akane said, as she reached for Tomoe who stood up to avoid her touch. "Let me talk to the head priestess. Perhaps we can make arrangements for you to practice with your sword."

"Really?" Tomoe asked, her eyes large and hopeful.

It was the least she could do.

"I'll have to ask the head priestess first, and you'll only spar with me."

Tomoe threw her arms around Akane's neck and squeezed her tight. "Thank you, Akane. You don't know how much this means to me."

Now she just had to convince the head priestess.

As soon as Akane exited her chamber the next morning, Shinon was waiting for her.

"Morning, I hope you—"

"Let's go," Akane said and strode toward Tomoe's chamber. She didn't look to make sure she followed her. She had bigger concerns than that nuisance to worry about.

Akane was distracted during morning prayer. How was she going to present the idea of Tomoe sword fighting to the head priestess? The kamigakari's body could not have a blemish. And fighting meant an almost certainty of injury. But Tomoe's discontent could just as easily transform into impurities in her soul. Perhaps if they stopped the training early enough before her ascension and took every precaution to prevent scarring?

"Prayers are over," Shinon said.

Akane snapped her gaze to her, blinking in confusion for a moment. It was then she took in the haze of smoke and the benevolent stare of the kami from her portrait on the altar. Akane shook her head.

"Time for breakfast," Akane said to Tomoe, bustling her out of the room.

Tomoe led the way to the meal hall. She whistled softly, waving to her friends. Guilt twisted in Akane's stomach. As Tomoe disappeared into the building, Shinon cut off Akane's path.

"What do you want?" Akane sighed.

"I wanted to apologize for last night," Shinon said. Her chin lowered to her chest.

"Apologizing won't save you." She held up her hand in a stop motion. "I'm going to tell the head priestess what you've done and then you'll be out of here."

"What's so wrong about the girl sparring? It's harmless."

"You hurt her!"

"Hardly."

"Who was hurt?" The head priestess asked from behind. Akane and Shinon jumped apart. The bent old woman looked between the two of them. Her hair was entirely white and thinning, her body was wrinkled, and her skin was stretched tight over knobby bones and covered in ages spots. But despite the frailties of her body, a fire remained in her gaze that demanded obedience.

Akane bowed much too deep for the circumstances. "Head Priestess, I was going to report to you—"

She held up her hand. "Come with me, we need to talk."

Akane made a sharp gesture to Shinon to follow, and the pair of them fell in line behind the head priestess.

"Not you." The head priestess had pointed to Shinon. "You follow Tomoe and make sure she stays on schedule.

Akane stared wide-eyed at the head priestess and wanted to argue, but the look in the old woman's eyes was too forbidding to even attempt.

They went back to the head priestess' chambers. She took a seat at her desk, groaning from aching joints as she did so. Akane rushed forward to help her sit, but the head priestess waved her away.

"Head Priestess, I'm sorry. I will watch Tomoe better next time."

"I didn't call you here to scold you, Akane," the head priestess said mildly.

Akane clamped her mouth shut. What else could this be about?

"You've looked over many of kamigakari candidates, haven't you?" the head priestess asked.

"I have."

"And since Tomoe has been here, have you ever seen the slightest inkling of power in her?"

"No..."

"I fear she may not be fit to become the kamigakari." The head priestess sighed and looked at a letter on her desk. The precise brush strokes were like a dark river flowing over the paper.

Akane twisted her hands together. "She just needs more time, some bloom later than others—"

"Have you seen any who show no signs at sixteen?"

Akane lowered her head. "Then what will happen to her?"

The head priestess reached across the desk to take Akane's hand. "I am doing this for her sake as much as yours. I cannot let you go through what happened to Mei again."

Akane winced. For a moment she was lost to memories.

The room was on fire and Mei was screaming her name. "Please, Akane. Help me!"

A cold sweat broke out over her body. That horrid moment replaying before her eyes in vivid clarity. She felt the flames licking against her body. Mei's pained screams echoed in her ears.

"Akane!" The head priestess slammed her hand onto the table.

The flames were overlaying the head priestess, and her eyes were empty black holes. Akane took a ragged breath, trying to keep the tears from falling in front of the head priestess. She stood up to pace the room, and after a few turns the visions faded. Akane's entire body was trembling as she leaned against the bookcase.

"I know you are fond of her, but she must go back to the White Palace."

She swore after Mei, she would see Tomoe reach her full potential. To come this close to the end and fail, it felt like she was betraying Mei's memory.

"It's not too late. Her power could manifest!" Akane said.

"This is not open for discussion." The head priestess' voice rose. "I told you because I know you are close. But you are nothing but a protector. It is not your decision to make."

Akane lowered her head once more. It wasn't her place to make that judgment. She could never be pure like a kami-gakari; she couldn't receive the kami's light. Though she'd sworn herself in service to the kami hundreds of years ago, as a yokai she would always be tainted, a beast, who by her very nature was impure.

"Tomoe's path will diverge from yours. A replacement will arrive and take her place. The cycle continues on."

But Akane couldn't help but feel like this was her fault. "Yes, Head Priestess."

Just then the door flung open. Tomoe stood there with her face flushed. "I won't go back there. I refuse."

"Be reasonable," the head priestess tried to say.

"How can you both decide my life for me without consulting me?"

"No one's life is their own, child," the head priestess replied.

"Well, mine is!" Tomoe's face was flushed, her eyes bright.

More than anything Akane wanted to pull her into her arms. Soothe her like she did when she was a child. But the head priestess was right, they couldn't risk her life.

"You're not fit to be a kamigakari," Akane said, her voice thick.

"But you said—"

"Enough," the head priestess said, her voice like a whip crack.

"How could you?" Tomoe took a step back; the full weight of her glare was fixed on Akane. She couldn't meet Tomoe's gaze.

She loved Tomoe like the daughter she'd never had. And in many ways, she had used her as a replacement for Mei. If she had been less selfish she would have seen that Tomoe wasn't fit. She could have returned to the palace and lived a normal life. Not be forced into a life she had never wanted.

"I won't do it." Tomoe turned and fled down the hall, tears shimmering in her eyes.

"Tomoe!"

She never could stand to see her cry. She had to explain, to make her understand just how dangerous staying here would be.

Shinon jogged toward them, but Tomoe pushed past her. Shinon spun in place. Her brows rose to her hairline as she watched Tomoe run.

"What's going on?" Shinon asked.

Tomoe turned around a corner and disappeared from sight.

"You were supposed to be watching her!" If Shinon had only done as the head priestess ordered, Akane could have broken the news to Tomoe gently.

"I was. I only looked away for a second—"

Akane slapped her hard against the face. Of course she'd let her escape. Who knew what she'd been doing while Akane's back was turned. It was Akane's fault for hesitating for even a moment to tell the head priestess about what she'd done.

Shinon pressed her hand to her reddening cheek. "You hit me."

"I don't know why you're here, but you've been nothing but trouble since you arrived."

Shinon blinked at her as Akane knocked into her shoulder on her way to follow Tomoe.

Tomoe had retreated to her room. Akane slammed her palm against the door.

"Tomoe, let me explain," she pleaded.

She pushed to open the door, but it wouldn't budge. She pressed her shoulder against the frame, preparing to force her way in.

"Go away!" Tomoe screamed.

What was she doing? She couldn't force Tomoe to understand. Akane pressed her head against the door, sighing heavily. When Tomoe was angry the only thing that healed was time. Nothing Akane could say would make any difference.

"What got her worked up?" Shinon asked.

She hadn't even noticed Shinon sneaking up on her. Akane rolled her head away from Shinon. She was too emotionally drained to try and send her away. "Why do you care?" Akane mumbled against the door.

"You may not believe it but I'm not a bad gu-er." She cleared her throat. "Girl."

Akane ran her hands through her hair and sighed. "As a potential kamigakari, she must have immense spiritual power in order to house the kami's spirit. Without it, the kami would destroy her." Mei's screams filled Akane's ears for the second time that day.

Akane pushed off the door and paced the hall, to outrun the memories. Shinon watched her, head cocked to the side. She made no comment for which Akane was grateful.

"I take it Tomoe doesn't have what it takes?" Shinon asked.

"Tomoe has shown no spiritual sensitivity, so she's being sent away."

"Ah."

A tense silence followed. Akane looked to the door, hoping Shinon would catch the hint and leave. Better yet, she'd leave the shrine entirely and never come back.

"Why do you need a living kami, anyway?"

Akane laughed bitterly. "Strange question coming from a shrine guardian." She didn't believe for a moment that Shinon was who she claimed to be. But she didn't have time to deal with her right now.

Shinon scoffed. "I just mean, it's not like the kami care about any of this. They haven't in a long time." Shinon sighed heavily, her head tilted back to stare at the sky over head.

She wanted to challenge Shinon and use that statement to expose her. But there was something in Shinon's expression that Akane could relate to. For a very long time she'd felt forsaken by the kami. Ever since Mei had died, she felt like the kami had turned her back on her.

Shinon blew out a long breath, then smiled. "How about I try talking to her?"

Akane pressed her lips into a thin line. "Why would I let you do that?"

"Look, I'm sorry. I didn't mean to let her get away from me, but she's deceptively quick."

Akane cracked a smile. When Tomoe sensed gossip, she couldn't be deterred. She supposed she couldn't begrudge Shinon that. And maybe she was being too harsh on her. She assumed she was the bad guy, but if she did work for

Akio wouldn't she have attacked them by now? Somehow she couldn't imagine one of his minions waiting around through an entire day of prayers without taking action.

"I don't think she'll talk to you."

Shinon shrugged. "You never know. Sometimes it takes someone who knows what you're going through."

"And you know what it's like to be a kamigakari?" Akane raised her eyebrows.

"I know what it's like to not be in control of your own life."

It was crazy to even consider. But if Shinon had been abandoned by the kami she served, maybe she could relate to Tomoe in a way she couldn't.

"It's worth a shot." Akane gestured toward the door as she stepped out of Shinon's way.

Shinon knocked on the door with her knuckle. "Tomoe, I'm coming in."

Again, there was no answer. Shinon pressed her shoulder against the door and pushed. Whatever she'd pushed against the door groaned. Then the door slowly slid open, giving Shinon enough room to slip inside.

"Uh, Akane, you need to see this."

The room was empty. Akane turned in place, as if she expected Tomoe to be hiding in the shadows. Her futon was folded in the corner where it had been that morning. The chest where Tomoe's kept her clothes had hair ribbons spilling out of it. More clothes and trinkets were strewn across the tatami. The white haori Tomoe had been wearing was flung over the base of the brazier and her red hakama pooled on the ground as if they'd been stepped out of and left behind. At the far end of the room, the round window was open. Tomoe was gone.

SEVEN

kane leaped out the window and landed silently onto the ground. As she sprinted toward the forest that surrounded the shrine, footsteps hammered on the ground behind her. Shinon came up along her right side and grinned.

"I thought you might want some help," she said before Akane could ask for an explanation.

"I don't need your help. If you had been watching her like you were supposed to, she wouldn't have heard what the head priestess said," Akane said, before racing ahead.

Tomoe didn't have much of a head start. The forest was a tangled maze of undergrowth. Tomoe would have had to wade through it, and it should slow her down. Akane felt confident she'd find her in no time.

But as the minutes ticked by and she saw no sign of Tomoe, panic started to set in. She scanned the forest as she turned in a slow circle. Dark shadows loomed in all directions, monsters of her imagination crept in close to her. Akane's thoughts swirled with all the things that could have happened. A roaming yokai could have cornered Tomoe, she could have tripped and broken her neck.

Akane's chest heaved. There was a boulder nearby with a steep fall on the other side. Very slowly, she looked over the edge. In her mind's eye, she saw visions of Tomoe's broken body smashed against the rocks.

Nothing but boulders greeted her. She let out a shaking breath. Where should she even start to look then? Tomoe was impulsive, but she had never done something this reckless before. What if the yokai who were kidnapping priestesses were out here?

"She's not here?" Shinon asked.

Akane spun around. In a rage, she lunged toward her. Her nails had elongated into claws, and she slashed at the yokai. Her inner wolf howled for blood. She caught Shinon along her cheek. Three thin cuts trickled blood. Shinon wiped them away with the back of her hand.

"What was that for?" Shinon asked, staring at the crimson blood against her tan skin.

She'd been a fool to trust Shinon for even a moment. She must be one of Akio's wolves. They must have kidnapped Tomoe.

"I knew I couldn't trust you from the moment I saw you. Where's Tomoe?" Akane asked while pacing around Shinon.

"You've got the wrong idea about me." Shinon held her hands up in surrender.

She lunged for Shinon again, who dodged. They spun to face one another. Shinon's stance was wide and her body curved at an angle to Akane. Akane feigned toward her left and caught Shinon with an uppercut that sent Shinon staggering backward. Blood trickled down her lip, which was already swelling.

"I don't want to fight you," Shinon said.

Akane answered with a howl as she rushed Shinon, barreling into her middle. The force knocked Shinon off her feet, and Akane pinned her onto the ground. Shinon pushed back, breaking one arm free and grabbing Akane around the neck to bring her to the ground. They rolled around for a few moments until Shinon caught Akane around her waist, and pinned her to her chest with her legs wrapped around her torso.

Instead of feeling the soft curves of a woman, hard planes and corded muscles pressed against her. Akane frowned, confused by the sensation, and ceased struggling for just a moment.

"Are you going to listen to me, or are you going to take another swing at me?" Shinon asked. There was something very familiar about this situation.

Akane clenched and unclenched her fist. "Let me go and find out."

The wind rustled through the trees, as Shinon sighed. And then she inhaled deeply.

"What are you doing... are you smelling me?" Akane asked, horrified.

"Do you smell it?" Shinon asked.

She floundered for a moment. Normally, Akane was hesitant to use her yokai ability in front of others. But Shinon wasn't a human priestess, but a yokai. Shinon released Akane to stand and sniff the air. Her head tilted back, nostrils flared. Akane turned to give a half-hearted sniff as well. Tomoe had been here.

"She's close by," Akane said.

Shinon's eye sparkled with excitement.

"This isn't over." She didn't have time to fight Shinon right now. She took off in the direction Tomoe had gone. All that mattered was making sure Tomoe was safe.

It had been too long since she'd relied on her wolf senses. It was like seeing the light for the first time after living in the dark. The leaves were greener and the tantalizing scent of animals teased her nostrils. Birds calling out to one another at the opposite end of the forest sounded as if they were right beside her. The forest had come alive. It was almost dizzying. She'd forgotten what it was like to be a wolf.

Tomoe's scent weaved through the forest, like a trail of breadcrumbs. And as she got closer, Tomoe's scent became like a glowing light against the energy of the forest and its inhabitants.

The tangy scent of Tomoe's sweat was intoxicating. Her inner wolf relished the chase, the spice of fear radiating off Tomoe. Tomoe fumbled over underbrush, stumbling as she turned and saw Akane approaching.

Tomoe picked up her pace. Akane was faster and she closed the distance. The trees tightened together ahead. There was nowhere for Tomoe to escape. Tomoe came to a skidding halt.

Akane, high on the hunt, stalked back and forth, blocking her way. Tomoe bolted to the right. Akane grabbed her by the arm. She twisted it behind her back.

"Let me go," Tomoe said, "You're hurting me."

Akane dropped her arm and took a step back. What was she doing? It felt like she was waking from a dream. The lure of the yokai power had almost overwhelmed her. She would never have forgiven herself if she'd hurt Tomoe.

Tomoe rubbed her arm. Red welts raised up on her pale skin. Akane reached out for her, but Tomoe took a step back.

"I'm not going back." Tomoe bared her teeth at Akane.

Her inner wolf, still too close to the surface, growled.

Tomoe shrunk back, her eyes wide.

Akane rubbed a hand over her face before taking a deep breath. "What were you thinking running away? You could have been killed," Akane asked.

Tomoe jutted her chin. Her eyes were red and puffy from crying. "You think I'm a child."

"It's not safe for any priestess right now."

"I can fight." She reached for a blunt weapon she must have stolen from the armory.

Akane sighed. Tomoe needed to face reality. She didn't belong at the temple, she had to go back to the palace. A girl with no training wouldn't stand a chance on her own.

"Be reasonable." Akane held her hand out for Tomoe.

"I am. I'd rather die than marry him."

Akane jerked her head backward. "What are you talking about marriage?" Akane asked. The head priestess hadn't said anything about marriage.

"My half-brother, by the emperor's second wife." Tomoe scrunched her nose.

"Wait." Akane held her hand up and shook her head. "No one said anything about marriage."

"When you went away on that mission, she came to the temple. The head priestess sold me to the Emperor's second wife!"

Akane shook her head, that wasn't possible. The head priestess was a good woman. She only had the interest of the temple and the priestesses in mind. Tomoe must have misunderstood something. "That can't be true."

"You don't know!" Tomoe shouted. "You're blind to the outside world, Akane. Not everyone is pure and good like Mei." She spat her name like a curse.

"Hey!" Shinon said.

Akane's entire body went rigid as she placed herself between Shinon and Tomoe.

"Leave now. Or I will kill you." Akane bared her teeth at her.

"But—"

Tomoe took advantage of Akane's distraction and bolted. Akane chased her for a few feet before tackling her and spinning her to face her.

"You're coming back to the temple, whether you like it or not," Akane said as Tomoe wriggled in her grasp.

"I won't be your replacement for Mei."

Akane hesitated, the words tangled her up inside. She thought she'd been better about hiding her feelings, but perhaps she was more transparent than she'd thought. It was true. Ever since Mei had died all she had thought about was making it up to her. She thought helping the next kamigakari reach her full potential would wash away some of Akane's sins. How had she been so blind as to not see she was hurting her only friend in the process?

"You were never a replacement. You're you, and she was—"

Tomoe slammed her elbow into Akane's gut and then slid out of her grasp and made a run for it. She'd learned more during those midnight practices than Akane had realized.

She jumped up and as Tomoe tried to flee, Akane cut her off. She threw her arms out to stop her.

"Please, Tomoe, come back with me." She held out her hand.

Tomoe looked away. "If you're only worried about getting in trouble with the head priestess, then run away with me."

Akane dropped her gaze. Tears gathered along her lashes. Tomoe couldn't possibly know that Mei had said those exact same words to her the night before the ceremony. If they had run away together, would Mei be alive now? Or would Akane's very nature still have betrayed her in the end? There was no way of knowing.

"Guys," Shinon said. She hadn't even realized she'd followed them. "We have company."

Two oni trudged toward them, wielding clubs the size of Akane on their shoulders. With a hand that could crack her head open like a nut, they pushed back tree branches. Their footsteps shook the ground beneath them. Without any weapons it would be impossible to make an impact on their thick scaly hide.

Akane had never come across yokai in these woods before. Especially oni, who traditionally lived in the mountains northeast of here.

"We've gotten very lucky today, three priestesses," said one of the oni. His swollen lips were encumbered by the yellow tusks which protruded from them. He was missing an eye. Where it should have been was a puckered hole.

"You stay back," Akane snarled.

She pushed Tomoe behind her. Faced with real yokai, Tomoe had frozen.

The oni laughed as he closed in. Akane threw a punch, aiming for his gut, but her blow only sank into his jiggling flesh.

The yokai laughed harder. "Stop. That tickles."

Akane backed up, keeping Tomoe behind her.

The yokai stalked closer, inhaling deeply and looking down at her with a menacing gaze. "You're no human." He took another deep whiff. "An okami? Why don't you use your teeth like your friend?"

A white wolf, five times the size of a regular wolf squared her legs and bared her canines. The oni with the missing eye swung his club at Shinon, who jumped out of the way before lunging at the oni. She had speed on her side, and while the oni was pulling back his club for another swing, she went for his jugular.

Tomoe came to her senses and picked up a rock, hitting the second oni between the eyes. He rubbed the spot where she'd hit him.

"You'll pay for that," the oni roared as he thundered toward them.

"Run," Akane shoved Tomoe ahead of her.

The beast inside Akane pulled at her last thread of control, threatening to unravel her. If she lost control now... She wouldn't let that happen. Tomoe ran ahead of her. Behind them, Shinon yelped. She shouldn't have looked back. The wolf lay on the ground, not moving, and the oni were hot on their heels. Its club smashed into a nearby tree, which exploded into a thousand fragments.

Tomoe screamed. Akane turned just as a man wrapped his arm around Tomoe's neck. There was something wrong about his appearance. The edge of his silhouette was blurred, and if she stared hard enough it was as if he bled into the shadows around him. He was carved out of darkness itself. His clothes, hair, and eyes were the deepest black. And when he met her gaze, she felt this crawling sensation inside her skull. As if he was rummaging around inside her head.

"Let her go," Akane lurched forward, only to be pinned against the oni.

Tomoe's eyes were wide and terrified. Something inside Akane snapped. The wolf she'd kept in check so long burst out of her. Her fangs descended, her claws elongated, and she slashed at the arm of the oni. He yowled and let her go. Akane charged the man in black.

As soon as she reached him, he disappeared. Akane spun around. She was half wild. He had Tomoe a few feet away. She ran toward him again.

"Take care of her," he said to the oni, with an impatient gesture toward Akane.

"Akane, help me!" Tomoe cried.

She reached for Tomoe, but her fingers grasped at air as a fist crashed against the back of her skull.

EIGHT

Shin woke with a foot against his throat. "Where is she? Where did they take her?" Akane's eyes were glowing red as she interrogated him. Her descended fangs pressed against her bottom lip.

"Where's who?" His head was throbbing painfully. That damn oni's club really packed a punch.

"Don't play dumb. You followed me back to the temple to kidnap Tomoe, didn't you?"

It looked like his cover was blown. "Do you think they would have clubbed me if I was in on it?" Shin rubbed the back of his throbbing head and winced.

Akane rocked forward, bringing her face very close to his. Her pupils were tiny pinpricks as they darted around.

"I don't care why they did it. You pretended to be a woman and snuck into the temple."

He had to diffuse this situation before she tore his throat out.

"Look, I'll admit I deceived you to get into the temple." She pressed harder against his windpipe. Nothing came out but a strangled wheeze.

Shin waved his arms, signaling for her to give him air. She eased back and he coughed. She was rather forceful when she wanted to be.

"I don't know who those guys were," Shin croaked. "I came here for you."

Akane grabbed the collar of his kosode and yanked him to his feet. The pungent scent of wolf was rolling off her. The power he'd sensed in her before was palatable and intense. "Give me one reason I shouldn't kill you right now."

"I can help you find her."

He hadn't the slightest idea who had taken Tomoe or where. But he was smart enough to know she'd do anything for that girl. This was the perfect excuse to lead her away from the temple. Though the idea of turning her over to Akio made him sick. It was either her or him, and she hadn't exactly endeared herself to him.

Akane narrowed crimson eyes at him. Energy uncoiled from her, explosive and wild. Even when Tomoe was in danger she hadn't unleashed its full potential power, nor did she now. What a fearsome sight she must be at her full strength. Too bad he'd never see it.

Very slowly, she uncurled her fingers from his collar.

"See, you can—"

Akane grabbed his shoulder and whirled him around to grab his arm, pinning it behind his back.

"I'll let the head priestess decide what to do with you." With a rough nudge, she forced him to march.

He was left with two options. Fight her and drag her kicking and screaming back to Akio. Or play along and hope he could come up with a better plan. Considering he didn't really want to bring her back to Akio, he was willing to bide his time.

When the red torii appeared in the distance, Akane's footsteps slowed. He tested her grip. Just in case.

"Don't even think about it." Akane twisted his arm harder.

A priestess sweeping the main courtyard paused when she noticed them, her mouth agape. When they passed she ran toward the dormitories. Shin shook his head. These girls really lived such simple lives. Seeing Akane bring in a prisoner must have been the most exciting thing they'd seen ever.

They passed by a pair of priestesses carrying a stack of scrolls. Their eyes widened. They weren't even out of earshot before the whispers started. Akane tensed again behind him.

When they reached the head priestess' chamber, Akane leaned over Shin to knock on the door. Then she fidgeted as they waited on an answer. Her restlessness wore on him and he shifted his weight from foot to foot. Akane tightened her grip on his arm. After a few tense moments, the door slid open. The head priestess looked at the two of them, her expression neutral.

"You've found out then?" the head priestess asked.

"You knew?" Akane and Shin said in unison.

The head priestess moved out of the doorway. "You both better come inside."

Akane forced him into the room. As she did, a small crowd of priestesses had gathered outside the door craning their necks, trying to get a glimpse. Shin favored them with a smile. An eruption of nervous laughter rippled through the crowd. Akane slammed the door shut, muffling the sound.

The inside of the head priestess' chamber was small and cluttered. Stacks of books and rolls of parchment were meticulously stacked against a wall. Across from it, floor to ceiling bookshelves, crammed with all manner of books. There was a strong scent of paper and ink. On her desk, beside a perfectly neat stack of parchment, was a brush and ink.

"Head Priestess, how could you let this okami into the temple? He kidnapped Tomoe!" Akane shouted right next to his ear.

Shin leaned away from her grimacing. "Could you not shout in my ear?" He rubbed the pointer finger of his free hand into his ear.

"What happened to Tomoe?" the head priestess' tone was laced with authority.

Akane forced Shin forward into a bow, along with her.

"I'm sorry, Head Priestess. Tomoe ran from the temple, and when I went to bring her back she was captured by yokai."

The head priestess stood. Her footsteps hardly made a sound on the tatami mats as she approached. Akane's pulse thrummed against his skin. She raised her hand to slap Akane.

Standing between them, Shin tried to block the blow, but she knocked his hand aside. Her palm cracked as it made contact with his face, and sent him reeling backward into Akane. The blow split his lip and sent blood trickling down his face.

It was only for a moment, but he felt immense spiritual power unfurling from around the head priestess. As quick as he had glimpsed the power, it disappeared. He stared at her wide-eyed. Who was this old woman? Apparently Akane wasn't the only one hiding unseen depths of power.

"You hit pretty hard for an old woman." Shin smirked.

They stared at one another for a moment, locked in a silent stand-off before the head priestess bowed her head. She shuffled over to her desk, groaning as she lowered herself to the ground. But he'd seen through her charade.

"Let him go." The old woman waved.

"Head Priestess!" Akane said.

"Don't argue!" She slammed her hand down on the table, setting the brush on her table askew.

Akane let go, her grip lingering. She took a step back, her feet squared. Shin felt her eyes burning into the back of his head.

Arms over his chest, Shin studied the old woman. "If you knew from the start who I was, why let me into the temple?"

"A man could not enter this place any other way." The head priestess readjusted her ink brush on her desk so it was aligned with the ink pot.

"He works for the forest guardian, Akio."

"Not by choice," Shin said over his shoulder to Akane. He wished she would at least stand beside him. Having her at his back made him feel like a knife was about to be plunged into it at any moment.

"Which is exactly why I let him in," the head priestess replied.

Shin quirked a brow. "I don't believe we've met before. How could you possibly know who I work for?"

"Do you think me a fool? It was too much a coincidence that an okami arrived at our temple gates so soon after she escaped."

Shin barked a laugh. She was a crafty old woman. "Are you in the habit of letting your enemies' people into your temple?"

The head priestess folded her hands on the table in front of her. "You let Akane ago, and I had a hunch you were not loyal. Am I wrong?"

"It looks like you've got me all figured out. But what is it you want from me?"

"Tomoe is not the first priestess to go missing. We believe Akio is behind the disappearances."

He cocked his head to one side. This was news to him, not that Akio was in the habit of sharing his plans with him. Not wanting Akane to be more suspicious than she already was, he shrugged. "I don't know anything about kidnapped girls."

"Pity." The head priestess sighed.

"You can't believe him, Head Priestess. He's obviously part of the plot." Akane stepped forward and pointed at Shin.

He'd done a lot of detestable things for Akio. He'd killed and he'd hurt the people he cared about most, all for the guardian's amusement. It wouldn't be shocking if Akio were kidnapping priestesses. But as far as Shin knew he wasn't. Lucky or maybe unlucky for him. This was his chance to get Akane to Akio. She obeyed the head priestess.

"I'll find the girl for you, but I can't do it alone." He tilted his head toward Akane with a grin.

Akane shook her head violently, her braid swinging back and forth. "I'm not going anywhere with you!"

"Those are my terms. Take them or leave them." He turned toward the door. Akane cut him off, putting her body between him and the door.

"You're not going anywhere."

"Changed your mind about coming with me?"

"I'm not letting you leave until you tell me where they took Tomoe." Akane bared her fangs at him.

"Wait." The head priestess' voice rang across the room with power. It vibrated through him down to his very core. There was power in that command, and it froze him in place, his feet unable to obey his commands. The only thing he'd experienced close to this was with Akio.

Shin studied the old woman, her face was wrinkled and lined with age. At the corner of one eye was a crescent-shaped scar. Her eyes had an ageless quality as if she'd seen millennia. She'd piqued his interest. If she was powerful enough to freeze him with a single word, what else was she capable of?

"The collar you wear, I can break it."

Shin's hand drifted to the cool metal around his neck. He couldn't remember a time when it didn't have a strangle-hold over him.

"I'm listening," Shin said.

"Find Tomoe and bring her back to me. In exchange, I will free you."

A warm tingling spread across his chest. He couldn't have heard her right. Freedom? Where would he go? Back to the dragon? Find Rin? His mind raced with the possibilities. It was all too much. There had to be a catch.

"Not that I don't think I can do this, but why the girl? She has little power. Why go out of your way to rescue her?"

"You don't need to make a deal with him, Head Priestess. I can get Tomoe back on my own."

The head priestess sighed, and then looked at Akane. "No, you can't. Tomoe isn't just any girl, she is one of the most powerful priestesses to be born in centuries."

Akane shook her head. "That doesn't make any sense. Tomoe hasn't mastered even the simplest incantations."

The head priestess stared down at her desk. Something wasn't adding up: the priestess' immense hidden power, the kidnapping, the girl who Shin hadn't sensed any power from. Then it hit him.

"You sealed her power," Shin said.

The old woman turned her ancient gaze on him. She looked very tired. There were dark circles under her eyes. "It was for her protection."

"But you were going to send her back to the palace!" Akane shouted.

"Only as a precaution. After we lost Mei, we could not risk losing another kamigakari. I suppressed her power and planned to unlock it once she became a vessel for the kami. But with priestesses being taken, she is in even greater danger. Even the temple is no longer safe. I planned to send her to the palace until the day of her ascension."

"But Tomoe said she was to marry her half-brother," Akane frowned.

Shin arched a brow. Now this was getting very interesting.

The old woman's gaze flickered to the bookshelf as she addressed Akane. "A fake engagement was arranged between myself and the palace. We believe there are those at the palace who have aligned themselves with the yokai."

She was lying. He had his doubts about the girl's power. But he'd sensed the head priestess' power, despite the illusions she cloaked herself in. He didn't care what she wanted the girl for, as long as she could remove this collar from around his neck.

"I'll bring her back, just take this collar off me and I'll be on my way."

"Head Priestess!" Akane stepped between them again. "Think about this, can we really trust him?"

"You are right. We are not certain Shin can be trusted. That's why I will need you to keep tabs on him—"

"I can do this on my own. Let me prove it to you!"

"This is no time for your pride and recklessness, Akane. Putting Tomoe in danger will not bring back Mei."

Akane lowered her arms to her side and brought her chin toward her chest. Her resentment rolled off her like a heat wave. He would have rather gone alone. It would have been easier that way. It seemed the head priestess didn't quite trust him, and to be fair he didn't trust her either. But he was willing to take a chance, if it meant his freedom.

"There's just one complication," Shin said.

Akane's gaze was flinty while the head priestess looked only curious as the pair of them turned their attention onto him.

"I still serve Akio." He plucked at the collar around his neck.

"You have my word. But in the meantime..." The old woman pulled an ofuda from her sleeve.

Shin took a step back. The tools of a powerful priestess could turn a yokai to ash.

"I'm not going to hurt you," She said as she hobbled over to him. Then she sang, the notes high and reverberating. The ofuda flickered in her hand, taking on a life of its own. Then grasping his collar, she wrapped the ofuda around it. The paper grew, stretching and winding its way until it completely covered the collar.

There was a bright flash, and Shin threw his arm up to shield his eyes. When he lowered his hand, perfect copies of both Akane and Shinon were standing in the room with them.

The clones stood eerily still, unblinking.

"The fake Akane and Shin will take over your places here at the temple."

Akane's eyes were wide as she examined her copy. This was advanced magic, indeed. If anyone had the ability to break his collar, it was the head priestess.

"With my binding, Akio cannot command you with the collar. Once you bring her back safely, I will remove it," the head priestess said.

Shin pressed the tips of his fingers to the collar. It was warm, but otherwise unchanged. For the first time in centuries, he felt the hope burning deep within him.

Nine

"We should be careful. The yokai in this region are ferocious," Shin said.

Akane kept walking as if she hadn't heard him.

Maybe he was exaggerating a bit. The crushing silence was starting to get to him and he felt compelled to break it. Akane seemed determined to speak to him as little as possible. She hadn't said a word since they'd left the temple. For centuries he'd endured the isolation of Akio's forest. Standing next to a woman who ignored him was worse.

He ran in front of her, forcing her to look at him. "Feel free to grab my arm if you get scared." He held out the appendage.

She turned her head away from him. She had to be the most stubborn woman he'd ever met. A large tree had spread out its roots into her path. But because she wasn't watching where she was walking, she wasn't going to see it in time.

"Look out!" Shin shouted.

But it was too late, the root sticking up from the ground caught her foot, and the momentum of her stride propelled her forward and into his arms. For a heartbeat, she stared up at him, her cheeks flushed with embarrassment and her lips parted ever so slightly. It was rather endearing.

"You know if you wanted me to hold you, you just had to ask."

She shoved off his chest and took a few steps away from him for good measure. Then, gaze forward, she strode away with her arms swinging at her side.

"You're going to have to talk to me eventually. I'm the one leading this search, aren't I?"

She turned, giving him a death glare. "I'm not stupid. I know we're going to have to speak. But I have nothing to say to you right now."

"Maybe you could tell me a bit about yourself. How did you become a temple guardian?"

She moved so quickly she was a blur of motion. One second she was walking away, the next her index finger was inches from his nose. "Let's get something clear. I'm only going with you because the head priestess commanded me. I don't trust you and I definitely have no interest in making small talk with you."

He couldn't hide his smirk. She had a lot of fire. Maybe a little too much. It really was a good thing he didn't need to bring her back to Akio. She likely would have torn him to shreds if he'd really tried. "As you wish." He gave her a mocking bow.

Her mouth clenched and her lips were pressed into a thin white line. A muscle ticked in her jaw.

"If you have something else to say, just get it out now," he taunted. He just couldn't help himself. Getting a rise out of her was a rather amusing way to pass the time.

Her exhale was ragged. "You're not worth the effort."

"To find out what yokai took Tomoe you're going to have to talk to yokai, you know."

"I can handle a few filthy yokai."

"You love lying to yourself, don't you? You play human, but you're just as yokai as me." No matter how he looked at it, her hatred of yokai didn't make any sense to him. Clearly she was a powerful yokai herself, though she pretended to be otherwise. Why hide it and limit herself to the position of temple guardian?

Hands balled into fists at her sides, she said through gritted teeth, "I don't play at being human. I am a temple guardian. I am sworn to the divine."

"Sure you don't. If you had transformed into your true form, then we wouldn't be in this mess, now would we?"

"If I had, we'd all be dead!" The words had burst out of her, echoing across the forest around them and startling birds out of their roosts. They squawked in protest as they flew away.

Now that was not the response he was expecting.

For a second her eyes had changed color. Power rippled out of her, and like a wave it slammed into him, nearly knocking him over. Shin's mouth hung open. The power she kept hidden was more immense than he'd thought. He snapped his mouth shut.

An oppressive silence fell over them. She stood stone still. The only movement was the slow rise and fall of her chest. After a few movements she emerged from her meditative state, and her eyes had returned to their usual brown.

He'd taken it too far. Perhaps he'd spent too long in isolation, and he'd forgotten how to talk to others. In a calmer tone Shin said, "Alright. Clearly we've gotten off on the wrong foot—"

She scoffed.

"Let's start over. Whether we like it or not, we have to work together."

"Just don't ask me again about—" She swallowed hard, her eyes focused on the ground. She took another deep breath and her gaze snapped back up to him. "I'm only here to make sure you do as you promised."

"Believe me. More than anything, I want this off." He touched his fingers to his collar. Whatever spell the head priestess had put on it left an ambient warmth.

Akane's eyes trailed over the collar. Most people avoided looking at it. Because anyone who tried usually got a beating for it. There was a hint of pity in her gaze. Then with a flip of her braid, she stomped away. It left him feeling exposed.

They ventured deeper into the forest. These woods should be crawling with lesser yokai: immortal creatures that had little more intelligence than their animal counterparts. Normally they were drawn by greater spiritual power, like moths to a flame. But the forest lacked any at all. The hairs on the back of his neck stood on end. The energy here felt tainted somehow. A dissonant note ran through the forest's pure energy. Like one wrong note played on a koto.

Shin stopped in his tracks and sniffed the air. He hadn't been mistaken, there were no yokai nearby. But what caused this crawling feeling over his skin?

"What are you doing?" Akane asked, arms crossed over her chest.

"This area has a strange energy; don't you feel it?" She couldn't be this disconnected.

"No," she scoffed.

Shin frowned. An okami of her power should have been able to sense it too. "If you keep suppressing your power like that, it won't end well." Energy needed to flow, like a river or the wind through the trees. Locked away and unused it rotted inside the yokai. It turned their very true selves against them. Shin had seen yokai locked in Akio's cells go mad from the lost connection to their spiritual power. Others became feral beasts losing all sense of themselves. That's why prisons like Akio's dark cells were so effective. Cut off from the flow of their spiritual energy, a yokai was better off dead.

"I don't need a lecture from you."

He shrugged and said nothing more. It was her risk to take.

The forest came to an abrupt end. The valley had been cleared out by farmers, and was zig-zagged with rice paddies in the hillsides. The setting sun stained them crimson, contrasting starkly against the lush green of the rice plants. Against the haze of a dying day, smoke rose on the horizon. This was what the strange feeling had come from. It was death.

Beside him, Akane gasped and clapped her hands over her mouth. "What happened here?" Her voice was muffled by her fingers.

Shin's nostrils flared. The air stank of blood, fire, and smoke. There was the stink of something else hidden beneath the carnage. Yokai. It was not entirely unheard of for yokai to attack humans. But normally attacks were on individuals who'd roamed into yokai territory. On a rare occasion a starving yokai might raid a village. Never before had he seen this sort of carnage. He couldn't tell Akane his suspicions, not until he knew more.

"I'm going to investigate," he said.

"I'm going with you."

He jerked his head toward her. "We don't know if whoever did this is still around. It might be dangerous."

She swallowed hard. "I can take care of myself."

They made their way through the valley toward the remains of a village. It was nothing but ash and charred bodies. Their arms were outstretched, bodies splayed as if burned while trying to escape.

Akane stared at it in wide-eyed horror. Her arms were wrapped tight around her torso and her body trembled. It hit him then how naive she was. She had likely never seen carnage of this magnitude while sheltered inside her temple.

"If it's too much." He reached out to comfort her, but she stepped just outside his reach.

"No." She choked on the words. Then she cleared her throat and said, "I can handle it."

They made their way through the village and up the hill toward the Imperial Palace. There was not much left but the blackened skeletal remains of the building. Bright red embers still glowed. A thick cloud of smoke choked the air, and Shin covered his mouth with his sleeve.

The paint on the gates was bubbled and curled. One had been smashed through, jagged fragments strewn across the ground. The courtyard was littered with the burned corpses of the servants and soldiers. The latter distinguishable by the weapons they clutched in their hands.

Akane's gaze was fixated on a dead woman who'd fallen on the steps leading into the courtyard. Perhaps she had been a lady of the house who'd been trying to flee. The corpse was not completely burnt, and her red and gold kimono stood out against the destruction around her. Her pale, dainty hands were reaching for the hand of a small, charred corpse.

"We should go, there's nothing for us here," Shin said turning away. He was unable to look upon the senseless loss of life. He'd seen plenty of death and destruction in his long life, but it never got easier. Yokai had done this. Beneath the bitter scent of ash were boar and monkey. This had been Akio's doing.

Akane was frozen in place, sweat beaded on her forehead.

"Akane?" he touched her shoulder.

She jumped at his touch. Hands raised in defense, she twirled to face him. "Don't touch me."

Shin held up his hands in surrender.

"I apologize. I didn't mean to startle you."

A growl rumbled at the back of her throat. Her appearance was more wolf-like now - her ears had shifted higher on her head, her hair grown down her face, her nose was more muzzle-like, and her teeth were sharp points.

"Make sure you don't do it again." She shoved off him and strode out the remains of the palace.

He watched her go, rubbing his bruised throat. What was that about?

THEY MADE THEIR WAY TO THEIR FIRST DESTINATION AMIDST oppressive silence. The sun had set by the time they arrived at the yokai inn. Lanterns hung suspended in air, emitting a soft yellow glow on the cobblestones. The building was multiple stories and impossibly tall. Any human structure would have toppled over. The windows, which lined all sides, were cast in a golden glow. Red lanterns dangled from the sloped eves.

Music and laughter floated on the air. A trail of yokai in bright yukata made their way down the path toward the inn. A boisterous yokai pushed past Akane, shoving her aside. Shin caught her by her tense shoulders.

"You alright?" he asked.

She ripped herself out of his grip. "What are we doing here?"

"Getting information." He gestured toward the inn. Akio had often sent him to this place to get information on the dragon. Shin was certain Akio wasn't keeping the priestesses in the palace, which meant they were being taken somewhere else. Inns were neutral ground and where yokai met. One thing yokai loved was to gossip. If Akio were behind the kidnapping and burning of that palace, then other yokai would be talking about it.

They entered the crowded inn. A yokai with shaggy hair covering his eyes and a horn protruding from his head sat behind the front desk.

"Welcome back, Master Shin," the innkeeper said with a bow.

Shin leaned against the desk. "Is my usual room available?"

The yokai bowed his head. "It is, and you have a guest?"

"Yes, and please bring a meal for two." Shin waggled his eyebrows.

"We are not together," Akane said.

"Don't be shy," Shin said, slinging his arm over her shoulder.

She slid out from beneath his arm before shoving him hard. He stumbled backward into a nearby patron.

Shin bowed in apology. "Excuse me," he said.

"Shin?" said a familiar voice.

It felt as if a bucket of cold water had been dunked over his head. Time slowed. Slowly he raised his head. A waking dream stood before him, a smile on her face. Her bright red hair was tied up in a pin and she wore a bright pink kimono. She looked healthy, happy. He couldn't speak. He couldn't think. He'd endured five hundred years of agony so that she could smile this way. The collar around his neck burned against his flesh. He covered it with his palm.

"What are you doing here?" Rin cocked her head to one side.

Words caught in his throat. Shin had sworn he'd never let Rin see him this way, as Akio's slave. She kept trying to reach out and over and over he pushed her away. It was too shameful to have her see him this way.

Akane looked between Shin and Rin, her posture erect. She reached for her bow but did not draw. "Do you know one another?"

"We've known each other a long time." Rin smiled and tried to catch Shin's eye but he studied the ground instead. The warm metal bit into his palm. If only he could tear it from his throat.

Rin bowed in introduction. "I'm Rin, and you are?" Her brows quirked and she gave a mischievous smile, as if Rin had caught him with some fling. As if the past five hundred years hadn't happened. For her little had changed, he supposed. She lived her life, married the man she really loved.

"We were just going." He grabbed Akane by the wrist and dragged her down the hall.

Once they were alone, she tore herself free. "What was that about?" She gestured toward the entryway.

Shin rubbed his palm against his face.

"Just someone I'd rather not see right now."

"Shin!" Rin's feet slapped on the floor as she ran to catch up with him. He kept his back to her.

"Go away, Rin," he said.

Akane frowned, and then realizing she was invading on a private moment, removed herself discreetly. He wished she would have stayed, it could have given him an excuse to not speak to Rin. Before he'd been Akio's slave, Shin had been one of the most powerful yokai in all of Akatsuki, second only to the dragon who ruled Akatsuki. He and Rin had both served the dragon together. And for centuries he'd watched over Rin, hiding his longing for her because he feared to lose the precious friendship they shared. Then she'd fallen in love with another man and he'd realized too late he'd lost his chance with her.

"Won't you even look at me?" she asked, her voice small.

It felt like a knife to the gut. More than anything he wanted to turn around, to take her into his arms.

"Rin, there you are…"

Shin's entire body stiffened.

"Shin, what are you doing here?" Hikaru, Rin's husband said. He was getting that question a lot today. He hadn't expected to run into Rin here. He had to salvage some shred of dignity. He turned to face them, a fake smile plastered on his face.

"Just having a bit of fun. If you don't mind I don't want to leave my lady friend waiting." He jabbed a thumb over his shoulder.

"I know when you're lying to me," Rin said, as the smile left her eyes. "Did Akio send you here?"

Shin ran his hands through his hair. "What does it matter to you?"

Rin's face crumpled. She wouldn't cry, she was much too strong for that. Hikaru put his hand on his wife's shoulder. Shin's eyes fixated upon it. He'd given up Rin so they could be together. It didn't make seeing them together any easier. That old, familiar jealousy squirmed in his gut.

"Priests and priestesses have been going missing, and we think Akio is behind it. Do you know anything about that?" Hikaru asked.

What he meant was have you been kidnapping them on Akio's behalf? It stung. But it wasn't a far stretch from the truth. He was Akio's dog, and had he ordered him to do so, he would have.

"Doesn't ring a bell. Now if you don't mind, I have things to do." He turned to leave.

"Wait," Rin called. "Whatever you're doing, I know it's not your choice. I don't care what he's making you do."

The collar was choking him, preventing any words from escaping. He wanted to tell her about the head priestess' deal. But he'd learned to hedge his hopes. If he failed, only he would know. And even when he was free of Akio, things couldn't go back to how they were.

Shin trudged his way to the room they'd been allotted. When he slid the door open, Akane was seated on a cushion in front of a low table. A meal had been served along with tea. A slow curl of steam rose off the kettle.

"Friend of yours?" she asked.

Shin ignored her and sat down. Sake would have been preferable. Despite that, he poured himself a cup of tea he didn't want. His hands shook and tea splattered onto the wood tabletop and left aromatic droplets.

He cupped the tea in his hand, letting the warmth seep into his skin. Rin's look of betrayal stared up at him from the surface of his tea. He swallowed the scalding liquid in one drought.

"Well, while you were out having a reunion, I found out where Akio has been taking the priestesses."

His eyes flicked up toward her. "How?"

"It wasn't hard. The maid who brought the tea in told me about it." She gestured to the setting in front of her.

"How could a maid know something I didn't?" Even now a part of him doubted the rumors. Could Akio really have been plotting something this sinister right under his nose?

Akane leaned forward. "Exactly."

She shoved off the table and headed for the adjoining sleeping quarters.

"I didn't lie to you." He stood up. After Rin's doubt in him, he felt compelled to defend himself.

She slid the door closed violently. The tableware clattered. Shin slumped back down on the ground. Maybe there was no more goodness left in him. He'd spent too long under Akio's thumb perhaps. Besides what did it matter if she believed him or not? Once they found Tomoe, he would never have to see Akane again.

TEN

Akane's heart raced. An oni stomped the perimeter of the encampment, dragging behind it a massive club. She pressed herself flat against the boulder she was hiding behind as the oni's thundering footsteps passed by. She peered once more around the rock.

The camp was squeezed into a gash in the earth, where an ancient earthquake had torn the land apart, creating a crevice, which had been further carved out to make room for crudely made buildings. Boulders were scattered across the landscape by some long-ago volcanic explosion.

The hairs on the back of her neck stood on end. There was the distinct feeling of being watched. The early morning light washed everything in a dull gray. Nothing moved.

She exhaled. She thought for certain Shin would have followed her.

After pretending to go to sleep, Akane had snuck out of the yokai inn in the dead of night. Though she'd known from the start she couldn't trust him, she needed to know where Tomoe was before she left him behind.

The maid's information had been good, and she'd found the yokai camp without a problem. When she got close enough, she just had to follow the stink, a mix of rotting flesh and brackish water. Underneath it all was the acidic stench of fear. They had humans here, she was certain of it.

From a distance the camp didn't look like much. A wide array of yokai sat around a sad, smoking campfire. Large brutish oni, like those that had kidnapped Tomoe, sat amongst monkey, boar, and lizard yokai. The latter were the ones who she had to be worried about. Their bites were venomous.

"You weren't planning on going in there alone, were you?"

Akane jumped and covered her mouth to stifle her surprised yelp.

Shin crouched down next to her, a grin on his face.

Her eyes darted toward the lumbering oni, who stopped in his tracks. He swiveled his head from side to side, his nostrils flaring. Akane held her breath one hand reaching for her bow and arrow. She notched an arrow and pointed it at the oni. His head was half-cocked toward them. She just needed him to turn half an inch more and she could land a shot into his eye, the only vulnerable place on him.

Then Shin leaped up from behind the rock. The oni growled and raised his club. Did he have a death wish? Akane drew back on her bow, the tips of her fingers seconds away from letting go. The oni lowered his club and he cocked his head to one side.

"What are you doing?" Akane hissed. "You're going to get us both killed."

Shin's clothes had changed. He wore the red and white of a priestess and in addition to that, his hips were wider, and his waist narrower. He turned his body at an angle to the oni. He had breasts that looked more like melons stuffed inside his haori, which was bursting open in a way no self-respecting priestess would ever wear it.

"Can you help me? I'm lost." Shin sauntered, his hips swaying seductively over toward the oni whose mouth hung open.

This couldn't work. Oni weren't that stupid. They'd see through his illusion in an instant. She shook her head and nocked her arrow once more.

The oni dropped his club onto the ground with a thundering crash. "What's a little bird like you doing out here alone?" the oni cooed.

Akane's mouth fell open. *You've got to be kidding me.*

Shin tossed his hair over his shoulder before pushing up his unrealistic sized breasts. "I was out picking wildflowers when I wandered too far from the trail."

The oni wrapped an arm around Shin's shoulders. "Don't worry, I'll help you."

"You're too kind," Shin said in a sickeningly sweet voice.

Akane shrunk down behind the boulder to avoid being seen. Shin glanced at her over his shoulder and nodded toward the camp with his head. Akane's expression was vacant as she watched the pair of them disappear. *I can't believe that actually worked.*

She wasn't sure if she should be impressed or terrified. But with Shin leading the oni away, a clear path was left open for her to get into the camp. She darted forward, keeping to the shadows and going from rock to rock until she reached the first ramshackle building. Yokai were walking about and she paused a moment to wait for another chance.

"Orders came in, we're heading south," said a lizard yokai in a low hiss.

"I wouldn't mind some time along the shore," hooted a monkey yokai.

"Don't be a fool. We won't have time to play. There's work to be done," grumbled a boar yokai.

"More humans to kill," said the lizard, baring his pointed fangs. Green venom dripped from the tips.

His slit, yellow eyes flickered in her direction. Akane yanked her head back to hide behind the building.

"Did you see that?" the lizard yokai hissed.

Their footsteps crunched on the ground as they drew closer. Akane's heart was slamming into her rib cage. The erratic staccato was almost audible. Her wolf stirred just beneath the surface. It was tempting. None of them were a match for her in her wolf form. But there was an equal chance she'd hurt Tomoe or other innocent humans they'd captured.

The lizard yokai's scaly hand, tipped in hooked claws, curled around the edge of the building. She reached down deep, drawing on the core of her power where the wolf remained locked away. It lifted its head, howling in approval. She felt the power flowing through her in a wild rush. Almost immediately her nails elongated and hair sprouted all over her body.

"Let me go!" Shin shouted.

The lizard's hand disappeared and their footsteps receded. Akane let out the breath she'd been holding. She slammed the door shut on her inner wolf. That had been too close.

Akane risked another peek. The trio surrounded Shin, who wriggled in the grasp of a monkey yokai. The oni was standing behind them, rubbing the back of his neck.

"What did I tell you about trying to defile the goods," said the monkey yokai that was holding onto Shin.

"But this one—" the oni protested.

"Shut up and take her to the others," the lizard said as he slapped the oni over the back of his lowered head.

The oni took possession of Shin and dragged him in between two buildings. And while all their backs were turned, Akane followed. Shin could easily free himself, though he continued to struggle against his captor. Or if he revealed himself, Akio's men seemed to fear him. But instead he let them take him to a large cage.

It was filled with priestesses whose white haori were stained with mud, and their hair tangled and matted. The guard opened the door and tossed Shin inside with them. As he did, Akane scanned the group for Tomoe, but she couldn't see her among the disheveled group.

The oni stomped away, leaving the cages unguarded. When the coast was clear, Akane crept over to the cage of priestesses. The girls were sitting in the mud with their heads against their knees. Akane's eyes darted over the face of each girl, while Shin knelt beside them peering into their faces.

"She's not here," Shin said, while still in his ridiculous female form. It was hard to look at him.

The girls were so defeated they didn't make a sound. Their eyes were hollow as they stared at the yokai in their midst. Akane wrapped her hands around the bars hard enough to break. Most of them wouldn't even lift their heads.

"She's gone. The darkness took her," a priestess said with an oddly melodic voice.

Akane pressed herself against the bars. "You've seen her? Where did he take her?"

"We all go into the void," she said before rocking back and forth.

It was pointless. This girl had lost herself to madness.

Akane leaned her head against the bars. Where did they go from here? Rage was bubbling up inside her, one that she tried so often to keep in line. She couldn't contain it and she punched the bars, splintering them.

A few of girls scooted away, but most of them continued to stare dead-eyed forward. The beast inside her was threatening to come out. She was losing control over it. The cage she'd locked it in long ago couldn't hold it back like it used to. Akane backed away, fearing that she would hurt them too. She clutched her chest, and a howl threatened to escape from her throat.

"We might not have found Tomoe, but we can at least set them free," Shin said, looking around at the disheveled girls with a smile.

A few lifted their heads. Maybe things weren't all lost entirely. His kindness surprised her. Not that it made any difference.

"What can we do? We're surrounded. They'd catch us." Despair threatened to swallow her up once more. This mission was doomed to fail from the start.

"Leave it to me. Go hide and wait for my signal."

She considered ignoring him, running away and not looking back. She'd raise all of Akatsuki if that's what it took to save Tomoe. But a handful of the girls got to their feet. Hope was shining in their eyes. Tomoe wasn't here, but Shin was right, the least they could do was help them.

Akane went and hid behind a nearby building. As soon as she was out of sight, Shin cried out, a high-pitched screech. The oni came running.

"What is it now?" the oni asked.

"Something. Oowww." Shin moaned and fell to the ground.

"I'm not going to fall for that," the oni said. But Shin was lying on the ground gasping for air, clawing at his throat.

One of the dead-eyed girls knelt beside him. "She's dying! You have to do something." Her voice had a musical cadence.

The oni glanced over his shoulder where his companions were seated around a fire.

Shin wailed again, reaching for the oni through the bars. He tried to shake him off, but Shin sunk his claws into his flesh. The oni roared and pulled back. A few of the priestesses rushed the bars. Their small hands fumbled over him, reaching for the keys.

One priestess was successful. She threw her hand up in triumph.

"Give those back," the oni hollered.

With his free hand he reached for her, but she threw the keys to another priestess who shoved the key into the lock. When the door swung open, the priestesses flooded out. At the same time, the oni broke free of Shin.

He cut them off, meaty arms held wide. "You're not going anywhere."

From her place in the shadows, Akane shot an arrow. It bounced ineffectually off the oni's shoulder. He turned around slowly, giving the priestesses a chance to escape.

The oni thundered toward her. Moving with surprising speed, Akane barely had time to even notch another arrow. The oni raised his club and the shadow of it fell over her. Akane backed away, her back slamming into a wall. There was nowhere else to go. She let loose the arrow aimed at his vulnerable eye, but he was too close and it bounced ineffectually off his thick hide. Inches from smashing her into a pulp, his club slipped from his meaty hand. The oni's step faltered. He tilted forward and crashed onto the ground at Akane's feet. She looked up from the unconscious oni to Shin who stood over him, rock in hand.

"That really worked. I'm surprised." He tossed the rock aside, with a self-satisfied grin.

Akane burst into laughter. It wasn't the time for this, but she couldn't help herself. Shin met her eye and they shared a private joke. Maybe she had been too harsh on him.

Their amusement was cut short. The other yokai had heard the commotion and came running. There were more yokai in this camp than she'd seen. Monkey yokai climbed over the tops of buildings. Lizard yokai crawled forward with their fangs bared. Behind them a line of boar yokai and oni squeezed in between the buildings.

Akane shot a series of arrows one after another. It took down a few of the smaller yokai. But when one fell, the yokai behind them stepped over their fallen comrade and took his place.

Shin transformed into his wolf form. She had to tilt her head back to take him all in. The white hairs on his back were raised as he bared his teeth in a menacing growl.

"Shin?" One of the boar yokai asked.

A concerned mutter rippled through the crowd.

"I'm letting these girls go." His voice rumbled over the crowd.

One of the monkey yokai on the rooftop laughed. "Akio ordered us to capture them. You have no authority here."

"This is too much. They're innocent."

The yokai laughed, their snorts, hoots and hollers echoing around them. "They're only human. But if Akio finds you here, he'll skin you and wear your pelt," said the monkey yokai. He leaned forward with a diabolical smile on his face.

"He'll need to catch me first."

"We've got you outnumbered. This is pointless."

But they weren't outnumbered. Yokai were weak to the spiritual power of a priestess. And in numbers they were evenly matched.

While Shin kept the yokai distracted, Akane turned to the priestesses. "Why don't you fight, try and escape?" She gestured toward the yokai.

The priestesses kept their gazes on the ground. A few had sunk back onto the ground, clutching their knees to their chest.

"Don't you think we tried? We're not strong enough."

Shin growled as he knocked back one of the yokai who'd closed in.

"You are the chosen of the kami. Together you can defeat them. Believe me."

They shared looks amongst them. "I suppose we could try?" the priestess replied.

"That's it!" Akane cheered.

All moved into a circle, clasping hands. Then as one they began to sing. Akane felt the power rolling over her, a tingle against her flesh at first. And then a slight burn.

Shin must have felt it too, because he turned toward her. The combined strength of the priestesses was building.

Their voices melded together until they were speaking as one.

The pressure of their spiritual energy was a heavy weight against her chest. But she couldn't look away. It was like looking into the sun, a glimpse of the divine light which she must always hover outside but never touch.

The force of their song brought her to her knees. The yokai were screaming, running from the purifying light emanating from the priestesses.

Shin grabbed her by the wrist, pulling her to her feet. The yokai were too concerned with saving their own lives to notice Akane and Shin trying to escape.

Akane ran as fast as her legs would carry her. If she transformed into a wolf, she could move much faster, but the fear that she might lose control burned through her veins. There was no saying what would happen if they did. To her surprise Shin didn't transform, and instead kept stride with her in a human form.

As they ran some yokai fell, too weak to resist the purifying energy rolling over the landscape. They writhed in agony before exploding into a pile of ashes. Akane's own skin sizzled, and she had to push herself harder to outrun their song.

Power rolled over the land, shaking the ground beneath her feet. Shin yanked her behind a boulder. He pressed her back against it, his arms encircling her. A mighty blast burst outward in a blinding golden light. The yokai screamed as they were incinerated.

The air crackled with power before slowly fading, like a wave rolling back from the shore. But even being at fringes of such concentrated power made her stomach churn. They needed to get away, or risk it weakening them further. Akane glanced up at Shin to find his face very close to hers. He craned his neck to see around the boulder. Then his gaze flickered to her. They jumped apart.

A line had been scorched into the earth inches away from them. Had the priestess' power extended further they'd both have died. As it was the wolf within her was silenced. The purification had weakened her.

The priestesses trickled out of the remains of the camp, their eyes wide as they stared at the ashes of the destroyed yokai. This was the power of the divine.

"Come on, we need to get out of here before we're purified by proxy."

"What about the priestesses?" Akane asked.

"I think they can take care of themselves, don't you?"

Akane gave one last lingering look to the priestesses. They had gathered in groups, with new hope shining in their eyes. They'd done all they could for them. She couldn't get close to them now even if she wanted. They were cloaked in a divine aura. Any yokai who attempted to get near them would be burned.

Akane and Shin made their way into the forest, putting as much distance between them and the camp as possible. But guilt weighed on her mind.

"You helped them escape."

He blinked at her. "What kind of monster would I be if I left them like that?"

Akane examined the tall grass nearby. A blush crept over her cheeks. She'd been wrong about him. He'd risked everything to help her. Even now some of Akio's men could have escaped and were on their way to report to him. Saying she was sorry didn't seem adequate after how she'd treated him.

Shin grabbed her by the shoulder. Akane's attention snapped back to him.

"What are—"

He shoved her to the ground.

A lizard yokai hissed as he rushed Shin. Catching the lizard by the middle, Shin tossed him into the grass. He took a defensive stance and his eyes scanned the horizon. The grass rustled as the lizard stalked around him. The lizard's green head popped up behind Shin. His fangs dripped with venom as he lunged for Shin.

"Behind you!" Akane shouted.

Shin rolled out of the way and the lizard landed in front of Akane. He shot toward her. She reached for her arrow, but he was already too close. Shin grabbed hold of its tail and it gave Akane the chance she needed. Not bothering with a quiver, she shoved the arrow between the lizard's shoulder blades.

Green blood oozed from the wound.

"Get away, every part of it is poisonous," Shin shouted, leaping backward.

It screamed as it thrashed. A spraying of green blood burned the grass. The stench was sharp and acidic. Then after a few seconds it lay still. Shin inched closer to inspect the lizard's corpse. He crouched down beside him, head cocked to one side.

"It's dead," he said, turning his back to the lizard.

"You saved me." Akane stared at him wide-eyed.

"You're welcome." He smirked.

Akane blushed.

Behind Shin the creature lifted its head. Akane couldn't move fast enough to warn him. And the lizard sunk its fangs in Shin's ankle.

Shin shook it off him, before stomping on its skull to crush it. There was a wet crack and then the lizard was still.

"Are you alright?" Akane asked, eyes darting down to his bloody leg which oozed blood and green venom.

Sweat beaded on his forehead. "I'm fine." His voice was deadly calm, which somehow scared her even more. "Let's go." He took a few stumbling steps then he pitched forward.

Akane rushed to catch him. "Are you sure? Let me look at it." She knelt beside his leg and reached to roll up his hakama, but he pushed her away.

"Don't touch it—" He choked and made a gurgling sound. His knees buckled and he fell onto the ground.

She crawled closer and rolled him onto his back.

"Shin!" She shook him.

"I don't want to die." He squeezed her hand tight as his eyes rolled back in his head.

Eleven

"Shin, stay with me!" Akane shook him.

As she did, his body transformed, a contorting of light as he lost control of his human form. A large white wolf, his hind leg stained crimson, lay on the ground in front of her. His golden eyes were rolling back in his head and his tongue lolled out of his mouth. Angry, black spiderweb markings traced up his leg. If they reached his heart, he would die. Normally a yokai could heal themselves, or at least slow the effects of poison until an antidote could be found. But both their spiritual energies had been weakened by the priestess' song. As it was, she was struggling to hold onto her own human form and not give in to her true wolf self.

Now wasn't the time to panic. But trying not to panic only made her anxiety spike. Her chest was tight. If Shin hadn't pushed her out of the way, she'd be the one dying right now. She had to save him. She had to find the antidote, but could she really just leave him here? What if there were more yokai around? She scanned the grassy plain they were standing in. Tall grass stretched out in all directions and a few feet away the serpent creature lay dead, a pool of greenish blood congealing beneath it. A few hundred meters away was a wooded area. There was a plant that was often used as an antidote to poisons. It worked with a yokai's spiritual energy to purge themselves of impurities. Typically, it grew near water. Akane sniffed the air. There was running water close by.

The black had crept up over Shin's leg and onto his back haunch. She'd just have to take him with her. Though she had greater strength than a human woman of the same size, Shin's size and dead weight wouldn't make it easy. In her wolf form, it would be no problem at all. But she couldn't trust herself. She had no choice but to carry him the hard way. Akane knelt down on the ground beside Shin's body, her hands shaking. When she was close to him the acrid scent of the dead yokai's blood and poison pumping through Shin's veins made her stomach turn. Tangling her hands in the thick white fur she tugged, dragging him along the ground by his front paws. His head hit a rock, and progress was slow. Instead, she squatted down, and with some finagling she pulled his front paws over her shoulder and onto her back.

When she tried to stand, he slid down her back and she had to start over. She was able to move forward hunched over and his back legs dragging over the ground. It was slow going and sweat rolled down her face and neck. The little spiritual energy she had left was being depleted by the effort. Her human form was growing unstable and she lost her grip on Shin's paws. Trying to catch him, Akane fell backward with him, landing on his chest. She rolled off him, and onto all fours. Akane beat her hands on the ground as she growled in frustration. It was no use.

Like a gentle caress, she felt her inner wolf stir. All the locks she kept on her inner wolf were wearing away. She couldn't save Shin and hold it back at the same time. Akane took another shaking breath. It had been a very long time since she'd taken her true form. When Mei had died, she swore never to assume it again. What would Mei say if she was here now?

The black marks were creeping over his rump and had even tainted his tail. Each breath came out in a pant. Sprawled on the ground in front of her, he looked so fragile and shrunken, despite his enormous size in his true form. He'd risked his life, not just for Akane, but for those priestesses. If Mei were here, Akane knew what she would say: save him, no matter what.

• • •

THE TRANSFORMATION ROLLED OVER HER IN WAVES. FIRST SHE was covered in thick white hair, then her back arched as her spine reformed. It had been so long since her body had changed, hardly used muscles contorted and stretched. The last threads of power holding her inner wolf in snapped as she assumed her true form. As the wolf emerged, Akane howled, her voice echoing across the forest. Birds screeched in fear and fled their treetop roosts. Everything was more vibrant. The forest was alive with prey, and she was very hungry.

Remember what you came for. She pulled the wolf's attention back to Shin. She trotted back toward him. The stink of poison was stronger in wolf form. More prone to impulse in this form, she took a few steps back, blowing her nose to rid herself of the stink. She paced around his body, circling, trying to override her animal instinct to avoid danger. Cautiously she approached, fighting the repulsion of the stench. Then she clamped her jaws upon the scruff of his neck, picking him up as a mother wolf does with her cub. She dragged him along, flattening the tall grass as she made her slow trek to the forest.

Beneath the shade of trees, a thousand different scents and sounds pulled at her. A deer froze, spotting her. They locked eyes. Akane dropped Shin. Her muscles tensed prepared to leap upon it. It bolted, and she followed it with her eyes. Shin sucked in a rattling breath. *Focus.*

Akane sniffed the air. At first everything was a mixed together jumble. Then, one by one, individual scents emerged: the musk of a bear, the fresh scent of pine and grass, and then, at last, water. She picked Shin up again and followed the trail to a stony stream where a thin trickle of water ran. Nearby was a fallen tree, hollowed out by time and other animals. It was here she left Shin, hidden the best she could manage.

She hunted for the medicinal plant for what felt like hours. In reality it was more like minutes. Time moved differently in her true form. More than once she got off track, following the scent of prey. Then when she came to her senses, she had to double back and resume her search.

The stream dumped out into a small pond. The plant she remembered fluttered in a light breeze along the banks. She tore the plant out by the root. Dirt fell from the roots as she raced it back to the hollow log where she'd left Shin. When she found him, he'd curled into a tight ball. His chest rose and fell quickly and the black had crawled up over his belly, reaching its tentacles toward his heart.

Mei had been a skilled healer, and often prepared herbal remedies by grinding them with a mortar and pestle. Akane didn't have any tools. She dropped the plant onto a flat rock and pulled energy from her core to transform. Her hair receded and her paws elongated into hands, only to revert after a few seconds. She growled in frustration. Then closing her eyes, she concentrated on the core of her energy. All spiritual energy flowed through the body like a river, it could be destroyed or depleted. Replenished by rest or nourishment. Akane pulled at the bare threads of energy, balling them together to give her enough to take human form.

When she resumed her human form it was less complete than normal. Her hair was white still and white wolf ears topped her head, her nails long claws, and a white tail wagged on her backside. She'd have to make do.

Taking a flat rock, she ground the plant into a paste. Mei had dried the herb and made it into a sort of tea. But there was no time to start a fire and she didn't have a cup anyway. Once she had a thick green pulpy mound, she brought it to Shin. Careful to not let any of the concoction to slip through her fingers, she forced his jaws open and shoved the pulpy leaves onto his tongue. He swallowed some and then gagged. It would be a bitter and unpleasant taste. She clamped her hands on his jaw, forcing him to swallow. Once he gulped it down, she sat back and waited.

At first there was no difference. Then gradually the black lines stopped their slow progress to his heart. His breathing resumed a normal cadence. Akane pressed her head against his chest, listening to the steady rhythm of his breath. The black lines closest to his heart faded, receding back to the original wound. She sat back with a sigh of relief.

His golden eyes were open and were trained on her. There was hardly an inch between them.

"I think you're going to make it." She cleared her throat and put space between them by getting up to wet a cloth to clean his wounds.

"You saved me." His voice was a rough croak.

She whipped her head around to stare at him. "Why wouldn't I?"

He didn't respond. And her entire face had turned red. Did he really think she was that heartless?

"I'm not a monster." She cleared her throat. "And I think I misjudged you..." The second part she said quietly under her breath.

From the corner of her eye, she thought she saw his smirk. It was hard to tell in his wolf form. She busied herself dabbing at the bite with a wet strip of fabric. It had already closed up, all that remained were shiny pink scars. Her fingers traced over the wound lightly. It was amazing how quickly he was recovering. Yokai really were nothing like humans. She rarely got hurt, but when she did it took no time at all for wounds to close up. But she'd seen humans die from infections of minor wounds. Shin shivered and she jerked her hand backward.

"Thank you. I would have died if you hadn't saved me." He tried getting up on all fours, but his body trembled like a newborn cub's.

Night was falling. Long shadows cast by the trees fell over them and the wind's bite was strong. She had been so focused on saving Shin, she did not even realize dark was nearly upon them. As weak as he was, the elements posed a new danger. His body could not fully heal if he got too cold. Not to mention, the potential for predators.

"We're going to camp out here for the night. So you can rest." She gently pushed him down so he was lying on the ground.

He laid his head on his paws. "I like it when you take charge."

She ignored his teasing because he was ill. Akane busied herself by making them a shelter out of the hollowed-out log. She laid out the few supplies they had and made a bed out of pine needles. As far as beds went it wasn't luxurious, but it would do.

"This is a rather cozy spot," Shin said, as he kept golden eyes trained on her.

"Don't even think about it." She fussed with a branch to avoid meeting his gaze.

"You need to rest as well." He didn't comment on her partial transformation, or her stubborn insistence to maintain some semblance of a human form.

"I'll be fine." She headed down to the stream to fill her water skin.

"Stubborn woman," he said under his breath, just loud enough for her to hear.

Akane spent overlong filling the water skin. She paced around the camp, trying to warm her own shivering body. Shin was right, her spiritual energy was depleted from the priestess' attack. But she'd risked enough time in her true form already. If she transformed again, she might wander off into the forest and leave Shin vulnerable to attack. The wind whipped around her, sending another shiver up her spine and she rubbed her palms against her arms.

"I won't bite, you can come closer," Shin said, his voice a gentle rumble as Akane stalked past.

There was no use being stubborn to her own detriment. The only place to get out of the wind was beside Shin. Akane crept closer, sitting at the very edge of their shelter. There was enough space for them to sit side by side touching. The musky scent of wolf enveloped her in its embrace. It reminded her of her old pack, lying in a heap together, cuddling close to keep warm. Her inner wolf stirred, not completely sealed away. It urged her to tangle her hands in his thick fur, feel the warmth and kinship of another wolf.

"I knew you couldn't resist," Shin huffed in amusement. His warm breath over her neck sent goosebumps over her arms.

"I'm only doing this so you don't freeze to death in the night," she said with chattering teeth. Half out of the shelter and sitting still, she was colder than she had been while pacing.

"Akane, are you offering to share body warmth to keep me warm?"

Having him whisper her name in such an intimate setting set her face and body on fire. She leaped up. *What am I thinking?*_"Of course not. I'll keep guard, you get some sleep." She paced away.

"Whatever you want," he said to her retreating back. Her heart was hammering in her chest.

The sun sunk below the horizon and the cold started to creep in again. Akane ran in place, trying to keep her body temperature up. A blanket of stars gazed down upon them. She'd checked the perimeter and spent the better part of an hour pacing to avoid getting close to him. If Mei were here, she'd have laughed at her for her stubbornness.

The problem was Shin was so very much a wolf, it awoke something in her she'd rather stay sleeping.

His eyes were closed and he snored softly. Before she could second guess herself again, Akane climbed into the tiny space and knelt down on the makeshift bed. Very slowly, she lowered herself to lay down beside him, their bodies just barely touching. His fur was soft as it brushed against her exposed neck. Her shivering stopped. Yokai rarely slept, but he'd taken a lot of damage and he did not stir. Sleeping would be the fastest way for him to recover. What surprised her was how nice it felt to lie beside him. *I'll just stay here until morning.*

Before she knew it, she sunk into a dreamless sleep.

TWELVE

When was the last time she had slept this well? She couldn't even remember the last time she'd slept at all. Wrapped in warmth and safety with the scent of wolf surrounding her, reminded her of long-ago eras when she'd slept in a den with her pack. They'd all curled up in a pile to stay warm during the winter and had hunted together as a group. Their songs filled the nights. Back then she'd been a wild animal, fueled by hunger and fear. Then the kami had found her. She'd made Akane, she'd blessed her with her light and given her this form, in exchange for her eternal service. And then she left Akane behind...

Behind her, Shin groaned. Akane jerked awake from her dreaming memories. His foreleg was slung around her waist. Akane froze. If she moved too quickly she'd wake him, and he would know she'd slept beside him. Very carefully, she slid out from beneath his arm. As she did, he grumbled something under his breath. She held her breath for a heartbeat as Shin rolled over. Backing away slowly, she headed over to a nearby log. She perched upon it and forced her gaze forward, pretending to have been on guard all night.

A few minutes later, Shin rose. He stretched, his hindquarters in the air and his jaws open in a yawn. He must sleep like the dead to not wake until now. She turned her back to him to avoid giving anything away with her expression. Her head was cocked to the side as she listened to him pad over to the stream's edge. Water splashed as he drank from the source. His scent was all over her, not entirely unwelcome. It evoked memories she thought long forgotten. She hadn't thought of her past life in a very long time. But if he got near her, he'd realize the truth, if he hadn't already. Would she have a chance to wash away the evidence?

"Hunt with me," Shin said, interrupting her thoughts.

"You've got to be kidding. We don't have—" Akane replied and turned to confront him.

He'd resumed his human visage. Water dribbled down his chin and ran in rivulets down his chin and throat.

She turned away from him not wanting to get caught staring.

"We're both weak still. We need red meat to help us recover and if we hunt together we'll catch something that much faster."

"I'm fine," she said just as her stomach grumbled. Then clearing her throat, she said, "We'll find something on the way."

As she went to retrieve her bow and arrow from where it was leaning on a nearby tree, he caught her by surprise, stepping in front of her.

"What are you—"

He cut her off by grabbing her chin and tilting her head up to look him in the eyes.

"W-what?" she stammered.

Her breath caught in her throat as her heart hammered loud enough that he could surely hear. She searched his face for a moment, as his golden eyes studied her.

"Have you ever done it before?"

"Stop messing around, it was cold. It didn't mean anything," she said a little breathlessly.

He smirked. "I was talking about hunting."

She blinked a few times before pulling away from him and stomping off into the forest. The blush was really burning her face now. "Go hunt if you want. I don't care."

"You feel it, don't you? That gnawing hunger inside you. You cannot fight it forever. It is a part of you."

She balled her hand into a fist but let it fall to her side. "That's not me. I'm better off without that part of me." He couldn't understand what being a wolf meant to her. It was a curse. But even that short time in her true form, coupled with her dreams, had left her with an itch, one that she couldn't quite scratch. Nothing bad had happened, so perhaps she could let her wolf out for a little while. There was no one here who could get hurt if she did lose control. She shook her head. *Don't be ridiculous.*

"Then prove to me you don't need the wolf," Shin said, oblivious to her inner conflict.

She spun around to face him. She was ready to tell him off, but the peculiar look on his face gave her pause. His brows were knit together, and he was watching her warily. Akane gave a defeated sigh. "What's the point?"

"Humor me." He gave her a mischievous grin. "There's plenty of game here, can't you smell it?"

She slung her bow over her shoulder and asked, "So what is this, a bet?"

"If you like." He shrugged.

She narrowed her eyes at him. They were wasting precious time. Who knew where Tomoe was or if Akio would be hunting them down after the attack on the camp. But even she had to admit she wasn't at her full strength. She still couldn't maintain a complete human form and the wolf was closer to the surface than usual.

"What do I get when I win?"

"Whatever you want."

She considered his offer for a moment, looking around the forest for inspiration. Before she would have likely asked he left her alone for good. But after yesterday, she could see the benefit of working together. "Very well..." She said slowly. "When I catch more, you're not allowed to ask me about my wolf form again."

He grinned at her wolfishly. "And when I win... well, I'll tell you when that happens."

There was something about his smile that made her body tingle. It had to be a joke.

"That's not fair, I told you what I wanted."

"I didn't ask you to tell me." He transformed into his wolf form and darted down the stream into the woods. "Better hurry up, unless you want me to win."

Akane shook her head. Though her senses were not as strong in this form, she was an excellent hunter. It didn't matter what his request for winning was, she was going to beat him.

She found signs of a deer straight away and followed it through the forest hardly making a sound. As the hunt took her across the landscape, over rocks, and through thick brush, she let everything go and lost herself in the moment.

A stag dipped its head to get a drink, directly in her sight. It was a beautiful specimen. Pulling back on the bowstring, she aimed her shot for a quick kill. Then a howl rang out through the forest. It called to the primal part of herself. Her inner wolf, already too close to the surface stirred. Then it howled in response to Shin. The deer looked up, startled. It flickered its head around. When it spotted Akane, it bounded away. Akane swore. Shin had done that on purpose. She attempted to track the stag down again, but any time she got close it ran.

Defeated, she went in search of Shin and found him in a nearby clearing, dragging a dead boar by the throat. His muzzle and fur were stained crimson with blood and his tongue lolled to one side. The coppery scent of blood filled her nose and the wolf inside her salivated.

"You're covered in blood." She scrunched up her nose for show. She craved the blood and meat like nothing she'd ever wanted more in her life.

He walked over to her and sat down in front of her on his haunches. He dropped the boar carcass at her feet. She stared at it, mesmerized. The wolf howled inside her, desperate to break free and to glut on the feast in front of her.

She turned away from him, as if that would be enough to fight the urge.

"Go ahead, I know you want to," he said.

She clenched her hand holding the bow. "I am not an animal."

"Aren't you? Because I was awake when you transformed. You're a powerful wolf. Why pretend otherwise?"

"That's none of your business," she said with a growl. Her fangs had begun to descend.

It was almost too much. Her spiritual power was weakened. That combined with the thrill of an unfinished hunt was still hammering away at her veins. Shin's scent, mixed with blood. Her inner wolf was restless and hungry. She couldn't keep control.

"You can't hold it back. It will only drive you insane," he said moving closer to her.

His scent was maddening. Desire and revulsion warred within her. "Stay back!" She roared but it was already too late. The transformation had already taken over. Her nose elongated and her face was covered in coarse white fur.

She fell to her knees as the transformation ripped through her. She rose up a snarling beast.

"See, now is that so bad?" Shin said.

But Akane was gone, and there were only the wolf and a threat before her. She growled and lunged for his throat.

Shin pivoted just before her jaws from clamping down on his throat. Her teeth sank into the flesh of his shoulder and blood filled her mouth. He shook his arm and threw her across the clearing where she collided with a tree. She was momentarily stunned. Stars danced in front of her eyes. When she shook off the pain she faced a large, white wolf. His feet were planted apart, teeth bared. The human was gone, and though she was tense with unspent energy, she knew better than to tangle with a wolf bigger than her and she backed up a few feet. When she was a fair distance away, she turned and ran.

Her senses were under attack and everything felt brand new. Even the flowers had a more fragrant aroma than before. She heard the water burbling in a stream that was up ahead and everywhere there was the prevailing scent of animals. The blood from kills, old dead blood, and also fresh pumping blood in the bodies of hundreds of potential prey. She craved it, wanted it more than she thought imaginable. But as she ran, some of her bloodlust dissipated, turning to a low burning flame in her gut.

She sensed him following her, but her instincts told her to keep running. He caught up with her with ease. She looked to her right and the giant white wolf ran alongside her. She bared her teeth in warning. If he wanted, he could tear her to shreds. But he did not come any closer and so she let him join her. He howled and she responded. The sound bubbled out from deep in her chest and expelled from her lungs. It lifted her and drove her to run faster and further.

The white wolf raced ahead and led her on a chase through the forest. They weaved through trees and over shrubs. But no matter how hard she ran, he easily outpaced her, clearing hurdles that caught at her feet and slipped through spaces that made her chest constrict with panic. He looped back around, waiting for her to catch up as she went around a gap under a fallen tree, rather than squeeze under it. Finding her legs at last and gaining speed, she leaped over streams and boulders, and surpassed the white wolf. The forest was hers.

He kept pace with her, nipping at her in a playful way. They chased one another through the woods playing a game of tag. He would let her catch him and she would snap at his tail and then turn and run leading him through tall grasses and through dense woods. He would inevitably cut her off and the chase began anew. When she was finally chasing him again, he led her up the hill through the trees and they crossed a river, wading in the rapids that tried to sweep her feet out from beneath her.

At the top of the rise, they reached a clearing. The white wolf was nothing more than a streak of white running through the green grass. He looked back at her with a wolfish grin before racing ahead. She howled in delight and pursued him. She met him at the other end of the clearing. When she reached him, he slipped past her and bolted in the opposite direction. She caught up with him and tried to pass him, but when she pulled out in front of him he bit her tail and she tumbled to the ground. As he tried to pass her, she brought him down along with her, clamping down on his leg and pulling him to the ground. They wrestled on the ground, teeth gleaming and fur flying. The game ended with his neck in her jaws. He whimpered in defeat. She sat back feeling triumphant.

The white wolf lay on his stomach watching her with his head resting on his front paws as she sat panting. Then he lifted his head, his ears perking up. She smelled it too. She stood up and her entire body was rigid and focused on the scent. The stag that had escaped her before wandered into the clearing. It moved cautiously but as of now, oblivious to them hiding in the tall grass. The white wolf did not move but she could sense the tension in him, the desire to kill. But this was her kill. She had pushed back her urges before but now she was free.

It raised its head, dark eyes focused on her. And then it sprung away. She howled as she gave chase. It ran through the forest, weaving in and around but before long she cornered it, closing in. It swung its antlers, aiming at her belly. She dodged his first attack and leaped out of the reach of its impaling antlers.

She turned around and came back at him, snapping at his hind legs which he kicked out and landed against the side of her head. Stars danced across her vision but she was blinded by her bloodlust and she kept going. Snarling and biting, she lunged at it over and over, relentlessly attacking. It slashed at her, gouging her side. Blood streamed from her wound but she was beyond pain. She wanted to kill. After several attempts she clamped down on his shoulder and it roared as she dug her claws into his neck and held on as it shook.

He threw her off for just a moment, but she came back in full force knocking it backward. It toppled over and exposed the sensitive underside. She ripped into the flesh, and blood filled her mouth. The deer gave a pitiful cry as it died and she tilted her head back and howled. It felt good. She felt alive. She gorged herself, filling her belly with sticky sweet meat.

She noticed someone standing behind her, and she looked over her kill and snarled. The man had a bow in hand, which was pointed at her. She snarled and the man fired an arrow which sunk into her shoulder. She did not think. He was a threat that had to be eliminated. She lunged for him and he turned to run, but he stumbled and she overtook him. He sliced at her with a small blade, but it made hardly a dent against her thick hide. His screams were nothing but a guttural song. And then silence. He'd stopped moving and then she felt it, the other wolf. She'd forgotten all about him in her hunt.

He stood a few feet away from her, watching her with wide, terrified eyes.

He transformed into a man and came closer but she growled, protecting her kill. "What have you done?" he asked.

Thirteen

Perhaps it was because her bloodlust had been sated, or maybe it was Shin's voice that cut through the fog. Whatever it was, Akane woke into a nightmare. She shifted to her human visage, but even shifting didn't wash away the blood or the mangled corpse of the man lying at her feet. It had happened again. She'd killed an innocent.

There was little left of him that distinguished him as human. All that remained was red pulp, jagged rib bones, and his hands which still clutched a pitifully small knife. Blood stained the earth around him crimson. Akane couldn't tear her eyes away from it. She tried to cover her mouth in horror and then she was assaulted by the smell. It was death. She stared at her hands, which were stained up to the wrist and her face and chest were all soaked in blood and gore.

"What did I do?" she asked, her voice trembling.

"I don't know what happened. You chased after that stag and I lost sight of you. Then when I found you again..." He trailed off looking at the man.

Her hands shook, in fact her entire body felt like it was going into convulsions. How could she have given over to the wolf? She'd been so careful for so long. Her gaze slid from the horrifying carnage to rest on Shin.

"This is your fault, you tricked me!" She shouted, pointing her finger at him. But she couldn't stand the sight of her blood-soaked appendages and dropped them to her side. Screams echoed in her ears; already she was slipping back to that horrible day. Akane put her hands over her ears but it couldn't block out the sounds.

He put himself between her and the body, and she lifted her head to look into his eyes. She expected to see fear there, or horror. The last thing she had expected to see was pity.

"Go wash yourself up. I'll take care of everything else."

She wanted to argue, to force him to call her names, to condemn her for the horrid thing she had done. She should be punished for being a monster. But all the fight had drained out of her. If she lied down now, she might never rise again. She didn't deserve to live. She was an abomination. A monster. Worthless.

Akane crouched down onto the ground, curling into a ball, resting her head on her arms propped up by her knees. Once again Shin didn't scold her or try and force her to do as he said. She listened to his footsteps as he worked. She could hear the slither of a body being dragged across the ground and then a scratch and a crackle. Smoke tickled her nostrils, followed by the sickening scent of cooking meat. Fire. So much smoke. Mei screaming her name. Over and over. *Akane, please!* She screwed her eyes shut but instead she saw Mei's bloody body torn apart, burning on the holy fire. Her stomach heaved as she emptied its contents onto the ground.

Hours must have passed because dark had started to fall. Dirt and debris clung to her. She'd clawed open her palms trying to escape her memories. Shin grabbed her by her shoulders, forcing her to her feet. She was limp as a used rag. She didn't have it in her to fight him.

He guided her to a nearby river. It wasn't terribly deep, but if she put rocks in her pockets and walked in, could she end it all? Akane knelt down by the water's edge and her blood-stained hands reached for the rocks.

"I can only imagine what's going on in your head right now. But Tomoe needs you. You can't give up here."

There was no point in trying to kill herself. She'd tried before, right after Mei died, but she'd been too much a coward to go through with it. Akane waded into the water and scrubbed the dried blood from her skin. She scrubbed and scrubbed until her hands were raw. But the blood just wouldn't come out. It had seeped into her soul, and she was nothing but darkness now. A killer twice over. There was no redemption for her.

She screamed at the top of her lungs before wading into the water and submerging herself entirely. She held her breath until she popped out on top gasping for air. *What have I done? What have I done?* She slapped her hand on the water's surface over and over again.

When she finished that, she climbed out of the water dripping wet and found a fresh hakama and haori hanging on a nearby tree branch. Shin had found her clothes. She shed the blood-stained ones and put on the clean. Shin wasn't very far away, he'd started a fire and was sitting beside it staring into the flames.

He didn't say anything as she took a seat across from him. But he was cooking boar meat over the flames. The flesh popped and crackled as the fat dripped into the flames.

"It looks like it might rain," he commented.

Akane glanced at the clouds gathering on the horizon.

"You don't have to do that," she said wearily.

"Do what?"

"Pretend like everything is alright, like I didn't kill a man today."

Shin stopped turning the pork and pulled it off the flame. He offered it up to her, but she couldn't stand the idea of eating. He tore off the flesh from the spit and studied the ground.

"It's easier to pretend, don't you think? Because when you face the ugly truth of reality, living doesn't really seem worth it."

It was such a surprisingly genuine sentiment.

"I didn't think you could be so wise."

"There's lots of things about me you don't know." He wiggled his eyebrows suggestively.

Akane laughed, long and hard, so hard that she cried. And he let her cry. Great heaving sobs, which turned into screams. Shin made no comment, his eyes on the flames. Eventually her hysteria subsided leaving her limp and emotionally drained. Akane pulled her knees up to her chest, wishing she could fold up into herself and just disappear.

"The first time I killed, I reacted the same as you," Shin commented. His voice was quiet, tinged with remorse. "It was back in the early days, when the world was new. I joined the rebellion against heaven, and it was a blood bath. I fought and killed those I had once thought friends..." His gaze stared at the distant horizon, perhaps recalling his own tortured past.

"This wasn't my first time," Akane replied bitterly.

Shin poked at the embers of their fire. "Killing never gets easier. But from what I know of you, I know you wouldn't have done that without reason. There was a weapon in his hand. He attacked you."

"Even if he did. I am much stronger—" A sob caught in her throat.

"I'm not trying to tell you to not feel bad. I know that's impossible. But sometimes you have to do what you must."

There was a haunted look in his eyes, the same she'd recognized back at the palace. And before she knew it, the words were pouring out of her.

"The first time it was a girl, a kamigakari. The kami chose me to protect her earthly body. I'd been doing it for centuries, and though I cared for them all I never got attached. I knew my place. Then there was Mei. She was beautiful, kind, and independent. A kamigakari must remain pure, she cannot have selfish wants, she cannot love..." She cleared her throat. "Her life belongs to the kami. But I loved her all the same, more than any of the others." Akane stared at the crackling flames for a few moments, lost in her memories of Mei. "Shortly before her ascension, she begged me to run away with her but I refused. I had a duty and so did she." She took in a ragged breath. Just thinking about it brought the memories flooding in. "The day of her ascension, everything went wrong. The kami rejected her because she wasn't pure. She'd been tainted by the selfish act of loving me." She clutched at her aching chest. "I didn't want to, but the kami's orders they, they..." she fumbled on the words and then put her head into her hands.

Mei's screams filled her ears, begging her not to do it. The kami's power had compelled her, the wolf had emerged, and she'd destroyed Mei on instinct. Akane tried to stop it but the wolf couldn't be tamed. She had watched Mei's slaughter like a spectator in her own body. It was then that she realized what it meant to be a wolf and vowed to never unleash it again. And now look what had happened. Tears rolled down her cheeks. Shin had moved closer to her and put his arm around her shoulder. It shocked her at first, but then she leaned into the comfort and warmth.

Mei's death was like a scab over a wound, pick at it and it would bleed again. And now that man's death would forever be carved into her heart along with Mei's. She wished she knew his name or what he had been doing in these woods. Perhaps he was a hunter or even a merchant. She'd never know. Shin held her until the fire died. His arms were an anchor to the real world. He pulled her away from her painful memories as he told her stories about his time before he became Akio's slave. He avoided telling her how he came to serve the guardian. But his old life was filled with light and music in the dragon's service. She'd never know yokai the way he did. She had been created to serve the kami and had only ever been surrounded by priestesses.

"And then one time Rin—" he stopped and cleared his throat. "Well, I must be boring you with stories of my glory days."

He had scars of his own he was hiding. Maybe that's why the words she'd never spoken had spilled out of her. He understood like no one else had before.

"Not at all." She glanced up. Without realizing it, the sun had started to rise. It was a new day. "We should get going." She slid out from his grip. As soon as she did, she regretted it. Facing him now she felt naked and exposed.

"Too bad we couldn't get more information at the camp," Shin said, stretching.

After everything that had happened, she'd almost forgotten.

"I overheard them talking. They said they were headed south, to the coast."

Shin frowned. "The coast." He looked out on the horizon. There was that look in his eye, the same he'd had when they'd run into that kitsune and just now when he'd mentioned Rin.

"I think I know where we need to go then."

AFTER A LATE START, THEY GOT BACK ON THE ROAD. THEY WERE making good time for once when Akane got the unmistakable feeling of being watched. More than once, she had scanned the forest, expecting to find an animal or a traveling merchant. But each time she found nothing. Shin must have felt it too because he signaled to her to stop.

They were in the middle of the woods with trees on all sides. Long shadows and filtered light drifted down from the treetops. Birds sang and wind rustled through the leaves. Shin turned in a slow circle, looking for their stalker. Then he froze in place.

"Akane, get behind me." He made a slicing motion to direct her.

"What is it?"

He pressed his finger to his lips and then moved toward the nearby shadows.

"Come out. I know you're there."

A man strode out of the bushes. Long, black hair fell around his shoulders and he wore all black. It was the man who'd kidnapped Tomoe. There was a massive ax strapped to his back. He wore no armor, but his arms swelled with corded muscles.

"Have you gotten lost, Okami?"

He grabbed Akane's hand and squeezed.

"Not at all. I was just about to report to Akio."

"You've got the girl, now hand her over to me."

Akane looked between the pair of them. Had Shin ever said why he'd come to the temple? She hadn't really asked. But it all made sense now. Akio had sent Shin to bring her to him.

Fourteen

"You lied to me!" Akane took a step away from him. The hurt on her face was like a strike to his heart. After last night, he thought they'd come to trust one another, but maybe he'd been wrong.

"Akane, I can explain."

She shook her head as she backed away. "Was this all a trick? You wanted me to trust you so you could hand me off to Akio?"

The huntsman strode toward them. "Enough of your games, Shin."

He reached for Akane, but as he did, Shin knocked his hand away, meeting the huntsman's bottomless black gaze.

"You're not taking her."

"I'm not going anywhere with you." Akane snarled and took off at a run.

"Get her," the huntsman commanded, and the monkey yokai who'd been hidden among the trees prior, dropped down and chased her.

Shin transformed and pursued her himself. In wolf form, he could quickly outpace the monkey yokai chasing her. But when he got closer, Akane turned to shoot at an arrow at him to deter him. Shin swerved to one side to avoid the hit.

"Akane, I'm on your side. I swear," he shouted.

The monkey yokai hooted and hollered behind him as they closed in. If they got a hold of her it would be that much harder to save her from Akio.

"I never should have trusted you." Her voice cracked.

They couldn't waste any more time talking. All that mattered was getting her out of Akio's grasp. Whether she wanted to cooperate with him or not. Too bad they didn't have any priestesses to back them up this time.

Up ahead, a river dissected the landscape, one bank sloped upward. A small trickle of water rolled through a mostly dry bed. Akane cleared the river bed, and then ran uphill. It would slow her down, but it would also give her the higher ground. Shin held his ground at the creek bed, while Akane climbed. His eyes scanned the surrounding forest. The spiritual energy of hostile yokai prickled against his skin, making the hairs on his back rise up. Shin was no match for the huntsman. He was much too powerful. But if he could bide time for Akane to escape it would be enough. He couldn't bring another person into Akio's twisted world. No matter what the stakes.

Akane reached the top of the hill and turned, drawing her bow to point it at Shin.

"Keep going. I'll hold them off." He nodded his head in the direction she should go.

Akane hesitated, her arrow drawn, poised to strike him through the heart. Shin turned his back on her. He trusted her to make the right decision.

The treetops rustled as the monkey yokai leaped from branch to branch, while the thundering steps of a boar yokai marched through the underbrush. Further upstream, debris blocked the flow of water, creating a large pool. If he could lure them here and break the damn at the right time it would send them downstream and buy Akane more time.

"You unblock the river. I'll cover you," Akane said.

Shin turned to face her and their gazes met for a moment. She'd decided to trust him it seemed.

The last thing he wanted to do was put her in danger. But there was no time to hesitate. Shin bound upstream where a large log had choked out the river.

The yokai broke through the line of trees just as he reached the log. They spotted him first and started in his direction, until Akane opened fire upon them. They growled and broke into two groups. Shin kicked the log, which moved hardly an inch at first. The yokai were grinning at him, their eyes hungry. He knocked his shoulder against the wood and a trickle of water was freed. He could see the whites of their eyes as he gave one final shove, before jumping out of the way. The pressure of the water behind the branch burst the blockage. Once it was cleared, churning muddy water swept down the riverbed, crashing into the yokai.

Akane disappeared into the forest and Shin ran up the hillside after her. She was panting for breath as he loped toward her in wolf form. Her eyes widened in a mix of fear and admiration. Knowing her complicated relationship with her wolf form, he resumed his form as a man.

"Thanks for that." He nodded back toward the river.

"I don't deserve your thanks." She rubbed the back of her neck, avoiding his gaze.

"Akio did send me to capture you."

She turned to him, eyes wide.

"If I was being honest with myself, I couldn't ever go through with it."

She scanned his face, searching him, and it left him feeling exposed. Shin turned away from her, he'd said too much.

Then an arrow zipped past him. A few of the yokai had made it across the river before the dam had broken. Shin pushed Akane out of the way of a second arrow fired their way, and it nicked his arm instead. The wound was shallow but bled freely.

"You're hurt." She reached for his arm.

"I'm fine, let's get out of here."

They ran. The landscape got steeper. Fallen trees and boulders made it difficult to navigate. Then their path ended at a sheer, stone wall. The shouts of the yokai called after them. Shin turned in a circle, trying to decide their best path.

"What happens if he catches us?" Akane asked as she scanned the forest behind them.

Shin looked back as well. Yokai were swarming the forest. Akio had sent an entire army after him. He must have figured out what Shin was up to.

"You don't want to know," Shin said, before offering her a leg up to climb.

Akane stepped into his cupped hands as he hoisted her to the nearest chink to grab onto. She scrambled up the side, and only once she was at the top did Shin follow after her. When they reached the top, she gave him a hand over the edge. The landscape was barren, and without cover before sloping back down into the forest. If they could get there, they might be able to escape.

They bolted downhill toward the cover of trees, but as they approached yokai ambushed them. They could fight, but it would waste precious time, the yokai's back-up would catch up in that time. Shin veered to the right, Akane following close behind. They were heading back downhill, toward a gap in the earth where an earthquake had torn it open. If they went down that path, they'd be backed into a corner. He had to avoid it at all costs.

Another turn and they were blocked by another group that seemed to have anticipated their movements. They turned again, backtracking, fleeing like rabbits. The forest had to be swarming with Akio's men. *What now?* But just as he feared, each turn led to more of Akio's men blocking their way and their numbers were increasing. They were herding them and forcing them into the ravine. There was no other choice. Into the ravine they went. With fallen trees and exposed roots, the place was narrow, not ideal for fighting. Akane drew her bow and arrow, but he saw her hands shaking, the nails turned to claws and her fangs pressed against her lower lip. She was losing control over the wolf. After what happened, he didn't want her to fight, not yet.

The yokai crowded in all around them, along the lip of the earth, and at the opening they'd just run through. They drew their swords and archers pointed arrows at Shin and Akane. If Akio had wanted Shin back, then he could command him to return. The priestess' binding must have worked, which meant Akio was angry. He could face Akio's wrath, but Akane had to get out of here.

"When I tell you to run, run," Shin rumbled under his breath, hardly moving his lips.

"What are you planning?" she whispered back.

He gave her the barest shake of his head and thankfully she didn't question him further. The crowd broke apart as the huntsman strode forward.

Shin bared his teeth in a snarl. Akane drew back her arrow and aimed at the huntsman.

"Stand down, Shin. It doesn't have to be this way. Give us the girl, she will not be harmed," he said in a gravely tone.

Shin growled deep in his throat. He didn't believe that for a minute.

"I'd rather not, if it's all the same to you," Shin replied, placing himself firmly in front of her.

"She trespassed on the guardian's land. She must return with us to the palace to face the guardian's judgment."

"This seems extreme even for Akio," Shin said, making a sweeping gesture to the army surrounding them. "I'll take my punishment for disobeying," Shin replied, putting up his hands in a surrender pose. He gave the briefest look to Akane, trying to communicate with his eyes for her to be prepared.

"That's not possible," the huntsman replied without inflection. He nodded to the line of huntsmen behind him, their swords held in front of them just waiting for the order, and then to the bowmen on the edges of the cliff with their arrows notched.

"That's too bad." Shin transformed in an instant and rushed toward one of the yokai who was next to the huntsman. He caught the monkey yokai off guard and knocked him to the ground. The yokai exploded into action around him and swallowed him up like a dark, living cloud. He couldn't see Akane through the press of bodies. He could only hope she'd gotten her cue.

Shin growled and then he lunged for them, engaging as many as he could. They fell back as the huntsman stepped forward. They had sparred hundreds of times. Shin had never won against him, not even once. But he didn't need to win. He needed to keep him distracted long enough for Akane to get away.

They faced one another as if this was simply a friendly sparring match. The huntsman pulled his massive ax off his back and assumed position. Shin threw back his head in a howl before launching himself at the other man. He did not move and Shin's jaws almost clamped onto his throat. Then he spun out of the way at the last moment and hit Shin's shoulder blade. The blade did not pierce his skin. He ran past, skirting against the line of huntsmen who did not move. He turned to face the huntsman. He had used the back of the blade on him. What was he doing? He could kill him easily if he wanted.

Over the huntsman's shoulder, he saw Akane scrambling over the rock fall. The yokai on the ridge had not noticed her yet. They were all busy cheering and hooting over the fight.

Not willing to take a risk of her being seen, he danced around, doing his best to keep their attention on him. The ax was heavy and moved slowly, and Shin dodged easily. It was a dance between them. The huntsman was a blur of movement, thrusting and dodging Shin's attacks in turn. The yokai stamped the ground and knocked their swords against their armor as Shin and the huntsman battled. And then Shin's opening presented itself. The huntsman had left a gap, swinging too wide with his ax, just enough space for Shin to sneak beneath his defense. He lunged at the huntsman but instead they got locked together, their faces inches apart.

"Akio asked me to pass on a message."

"And what's that," he growled.

"You will never return to the dragon."

The huntsman pushed him backward with a foot to his chest. Shin was pinned to the ground. The huntsman raised his ax. This was it. The moment he died. At last he would be free.

FIFTEEN

Akane fled. Her heart hammered in her chest. The shouts of the yokai echoed all around her. Their menacing voices rang in her ears. The wolf inside her stirred, woken by her panic and fear.

She glanced over her shoulder, expecting to see Shin following after her. But he wasn't there. The wind whistled through the trees. She kept on running, a few more feet again checking over her shoulder, but once more he wasn't there. The treetops rustled and the voices of her pursuers grew closer. They'd be upon her any moment, she couldn't keep wasting time.

He'd given her a chance to escape by sacrificing himself. Tomoe was counting on her, and if she left now she could continue her search. But what happened to Shin? What would Akio do when he had him in his clutches once more? But the look on his face when he told her he couldn't let Akio have her. It haunted her.

She headed back in the direction she had come. The wolf inside her was pressing against her bindings. She felt the brush of the raw power against her skin. The tingle of gooseflesh. She was standing at the edge of a precipice. If she took hold of that power, they might have a fighting chance. But the odds were just as likely she'd lose all control and hurt another innocent. She'd have to fight without it. She just had to come up with a plan.

The musky scent of monkey yokai wafted toward her. Akane slowed her pace, eyes scanning the forest. Her bow and arrow pointed at the canopy of trees overhead.

Eerie, disembodied laughter filtered down through the treetops.

"What fun is it if you don't run?" said a monkey yokai from somewhere above her.

Akane backed away, head swiveling back and forth. She couldn't place where the sounds were coming from.

Branches rustled to her left, and she shot an arrow in that direction. The arrow sailed through the air, landing harmlessly on the ground a few feet away.

The hooting laughter echoed around her.

"You think your arrows will be enough to protect you?" They taunted.

If she unleashed her inner wolf, she could trace their scent and tear them apart with ease. Her wolf stretched and growled within her, eager for the hunt. Instead she turned and ran.

The forest was a twisted labyrinth of branches and undergrowth. It all started to blend together as she ran, just a blur of green. The echoing laughter of the monkey yokai followed her as she fled. One dropped down in her path, and she came to a skidding stop before making a quick turn to run in a different direction. She slipped on decaying plant matter and her quiver slammed into her back. It was slowing her down. She slid it off and dropped it on the ground as she ran through the forest.

Branches tore at her clothes and her hair came loose from the ponytail. With every turn she made, the monkeys were there in front of her. Their jeering yellow teeth smiled and taunted her.

Akane ran until she came up short along a cliff side. The drop over led into a steep ravine, the bottom of which was obscured by a thick mist. She eyed the distance to the other side. If she had enough speed, perhaps she could leap over. She ran back the way she came but stopped dead in her tracks as the monkey yokai dropped down from the trees. There were four of them, armed in leather and with swords at their hips.

Akane's back was to the ravine. There was nowhere else to run. Her inner wolf roared. On impulse she reached for her quiver, forgetting she'd left it behind. One by one the tethers she used to hold her inner wolf in check were being severed. Thick hairs sprouted along her neck and cheeks, her fangs descended and pressed against her bottom lip. There was an ache in her chest, a desperate desire to use her power. But as she imagined it, she also saw the innocent human she'd murdered in cold blood. Or Mei's desperate cries as she was torn apart.

"There's nowhere left to run, pup. Come with us quietly and maybe Akio will let you live." The monkey lackeys laughed at the leader's joke.

Akane closed her eyes. She couldn't do it, not even when her back was against the wall.

The monkeys closed in, coming closer to her. As they did, she swung with her fist. It knocked one off balance and he stumbled back a few feet.

"You bitch," he growled. And then he and his friends came at her all at once. She swung again, landing a punch, but at the same time another yokai grabbed her other arm. She kicked him in the groin and he dropped her. She stumbled, trying to break free, only to be grabbed from behind with her arms pinned to her back.

She kicked off the ground and slammed her head into its chin. He loosened his grip and Akane made another run for it. But more yokai dropped from the treetops. There were too many of them for her to fight on her own. Akane stood in the center, hands raised in a defensive pose, ready to take them all on at once if she must.

An arrow came zooming by. But it was no average arrow. It hummed with spiritual power, glowing green as it slammed into the chest of a yokai, who caught flame. It burned up in green energy before combusting into dust.

Akane spun just as a kitsune leaped amongst the monkey yokai and tore them apart, tossing three over the ravine's edge. The remaining few scattered to the wind, leaving Akane standing to face the nine-tailed Kitsune and the priest with the glowing green energy.

"Are you alright?" the kitsune asked, transforming from a nine-tailed fox to a woman with auburn hair and a pair of fox ears perched on top of her head.

The wolf inside her was raring for a fight. "What are you doing here?" Akane snapped. This was the same woman Shin had met in the inn. The one he'd been very desperate to avoid.

Rin held her hands up in a defensive pose. Just because they'd saved her from Akio's men didn't mean they were on her side. What self-respecting priest traveled with a yokai?

"We don't mean you any harm," the strange priest said, holding his hands up in a surrender pose.

"We sensed you could need some help." He tilted his head to the side. "Have we met before?"

"You're that woman from the inn. You were there with Shin," the kitsune said in a cheery voice. Her smile spread across her entire face and her eyes twinkled.

A blush burned across Akane's face. She felt compelled to clarify. "It wasn't anything like you're thinking."

"What did you think I was thinking?" The kitsune's brows rose toward her hairline.

Akane cleared her throat. Now wasn't the time for this. Shin was still in danger.

"Thank you for saving me, but now I have to go." Akane turned to brush past him.

"Please, before you go, perhaps you could pass a message to Shin for me."

Akane's footsteps faltered. What was between this woman and Shin, and why did he seem so determined to get away from her? She supposed it wasn't really her business. But if it hadn't been for them, she wouldn't have escaped Akio's men. She couldn't take on Akio's men alone. She turned back to the kitsune.

"Why don't you tell him yourself? Akio's men have him and I was on my way to rescue him."

They jumped to action without question. Akane led them back to the gorge where Shin was in the middle of fighting the huntsman. The two opponents were circling one another. Shin was outmatched and struggled to keep up with the more powerful yokai. He stumbled backward, falling onto his back and pinned beneath the huntsman's foot. He raised his ax.

Without thinking, Akane took the bow and arrow from the priest. She pointed it at the huntsman. It zoomed from her fingertips, burning like a green shooting star. It struck true and hit the huntsman's wrist.

The huntsman dropped the ax, letting it fall, inches from Shin. The huntsman looked up toward Akane on the ridge.

Her hands were burned from touching the items of a priest, which were imbued with spiritual power. She dropped them on the ground and went to pick up a nearby rock. She threw it toward a group of yokai on the ground.

"Get them," the huntsman commanded, his arm sweeping in their direction.

The kitsune transformed, leaping down from the ledge and into the fray. She cut a path through the surging group of yokai, knocking them aside like child's toys. The priest resumed shooting holy arrows in rapid succession down upon the yokai that didn't fall beneath the force of the kitsune.

Akane followed the kitsune down, fighting her way through the crowd. Shin too was making his way through the group. He and the huntsman were separated by the crowd, but he was wading closer to Shin.

Shin caught up to her and grabbed her by the shoulders. The sudden familiar touch stunned her.

"Are you crazy? I was giving you a chance to escape."

"And leave you to be dragged back to your master?" Her face was flushed as she shouted.

His eyes were wide and his expression difficult to read. But the moment was cut short when the huntsman cut through the crowd to reach them. Shin pushed her behind him, preparing to defend her against the huntsman's swinging ax. But before he could strike them, the kitsune leaped up from behind them and knocked the huntsman down on the ground.

"Go," she growled.

Shin stared at her in a daze. "I can't leave you to fight alone."

"Hikaru is covering for me, get out of here," she growled.

The huntsman knocked her back and lurched toward Shin and Akane, only to be blocked once more by the kitsune. Flames rose up along her feet, and Akane could feel the heat of it upon her face.

Up on the ridge, the priest fired spiritually imbued arrows to distract and slow the huntsman.

Shin lingered a moment, and he looked like he was going to stay behind. Akane grabbed his hand and pulled him away. This was their chance to escape. He resisted her momentarily, before following after as they fought their way out of the gorge. Once they reached the edge, they scrambled over the side and back to the safety of the ledge.

"Watch Akane, I'm going back for Rin," Shin said to the priest, as soon as they reached the top.

"No need, she's on her way." The priest nodded. Rin was bounding over the group, making her way back to them.

"You'll need to get clear. I'm going to purify them," the priest said.

Akane didn't need to be told twice and bolted for the cover of the forest, Shin hot on her trail. She heard his song rising on the ridge. It had the same power as multiple priestesses. Who was this man who had such power?

She didn't have time to question it. They ran as far and as fast as they could until Shin put his hand on her shoulder, slowing her to a stop. He tilted his head to one side, listening to the forest around them.

"I think we're safe."

She hadn't realized it before now, but they were still holding hands. She ripped her hand free of his and paced away from him by a few steps.

"You shouldn't have done that."

"Save your life? You have a weird way of showing your gratitude," he said smugly.

She spun to face him. "You were going to sacrifice yourself to that monster for me. What's the use of that?"

He stared at her, mouth hanging open. If she was being honest, before she'd been touched. But when he'd almost turned back for the kitsune, she realized it had to be something he did for everyone. He was just a reckless fool. There was no reason to feel special or significant.

"Were you worried about me?" He grinned as he leaned closer to her.

She harrumphed and turned her back on him. "I need you to help me find Tomoe, that's all."

He ran around to the front, forcing her to face him. "You were worried about me," he teased.

She pressed her lips together to keep herself from laughing. It was a relief. If that priest and kitsune hadn't found her when they did, she wasn't sure she could have saved Shin on her own.

"There you are," the kitsune said as she approached them.

Shin's smile dropped, and his muscles clenched. The sudden change in demeanor was like seeing the shutters close on his expression.

"What are you doing here, Rin?" he asked, his voice bordering on a growl.

The kitsune's steps didn't falter. "It was just a coincidence. I ran into your friend."

"Well, thanks, we should be going."

"Wait, can't we talk? Isn't that the least you could do after I saved your life?"

"Don't you think we're even?" he said coolly with his back to her.

"I know where you can find the girl you're looking for."

Akane turned to look at the kitsune, but she only had eyes on Shin, who stubbornly wouldn't look at her.

Shin was going to deny her help, but Akane spoke up before he could. "Where is she?"

Shin glared at her before marching off in the woods.

"I'll tell you if he'll talk to me." The Kitsune nodded toward Shin.

Sixteen

Was Rin trying to torture him? Or was this a twisted game to her? Shin stalked in the forest while Rin and Akane talked. Their voices floated toward him, their gentle murmurs caressed his ears. Hikaru had not joined them, but he could feel his spiritual pressure nearby. The intense burst of holy energy meant he couldn't come near them until he'd shed the holy energy that would weaken the yokai.

Shin paced in the forest. He wanted to run, to escape Rin's casual glances in his direction. To get away from the talk he knew she wanted to have. How she had learned that he was searching for the girl was beyond him. But he couldn't face her, not after she'd come to his rescue. Despite pushing her away for centuries, she kept coming back to him.

Akane detached herself from Rin and came toward him. He ceased his pacing, but his foot continued to tap on the ground.

"Ready to go?" he asked gruffly.

"She won't give me all the details, not until you talk to her," she said flatly. Her brows were pinched together in a scowl.

Akane's lips were pressed in a firm line, arms crossed over her chest. Hair fell loose from her braid and across her face. If he refused to talk, then Akane would be furious. It was just like Rin, to try and corner him this way. What would be worse, facing Akane's anger and distrust or looking into the face of Rin?

"You're not seriously considering turning it down? This is the exact lead we need."

Shin sighed and ran his hands through his hair. "It's complicated is all."

"I don't see how it's that complicated. You want your free-dom, don't you?"

He wanted to glare at her or argue her point. But she was right. It was his pride that held him back. He was nothing but a shadow of the man he'd been. A dog on a leash, almost defeated once again by Akio's machinations if Rin hadn't come to his rescue. It rubbed him the wrong way.

Akane's glare could set him ablaze. He supposed this time it was better to cede to reason rather than his bruised ego.

He heaved a heavy sigh. "Alright."

His feet were heavy as he approached Rin. He couldn't figure out what to do with his hands, fold them in front of himself or behind his back. He settled on leaving them resting at his side.

"Where is she?" he asked, then cleared his throat and studied the forest around them, pretending the bark of a nearby tree was of intense interest. As it was, he could feel her eyes boring a hole into the side of his head. He knew if he looked her in the eye, she'd beg him with those soulful eyes to return to the way things were. But they couldn't go back. Not now, perhaps not ever.

"Do you think it's going to be that easy, after the way you left me at the inn?" Her laughter was lilting. This was all a joke to her.

Shin sighed. "What do you want me to say?"

"I don't want you to say anything. I just want my friend back." Rin reached out to touch him, but he stepped out of her grasp.

The word friend rippled through him, the old wound opened to bleed again. That was the problem, he would never be anything but a friend to her. He'd loved her almost his entire life, but she'd never feel the same way. And maybe that's part of the reason he'd stayed away - because he couldn't face that fact. It hurt too much. He'd chosen to be Akio's slave rather than watch her give her heart to another.

"We can't change the past," he said.

Akane was standing nearby, her back to them, trying to avoid looking like she was listening in. But she glanced over her shoulder and their eyes met. She turned her head away quickly. Shin couldn't help the smile that came to his lips.

"I know I can't erase the last five hundred years. Or what you've been through. But we can rewrite the future. The dragon is rebuilding his kingdom. You could—"

"Don't—" He held up his hand.

Rin bit her bottom lip, but he knew she wanted to say more. But even once he was free, he couldn't go back to the dragon. He'd betrayed his old friend, and the dragon didn't forgive so easily. Like he said, there was no returning to the past.

Rin sighed, seeing that she couldn't get through his barrier. "I asked around at the inn. There's a temple in the mountains to the south that Akio has been bringing priestesses to. If the girl is anywhere, it's there."

"Thanks." He turned to walk away.

"Shin, think about the offer at least."

He didn't acknowledge her words as he walked toward Akane. She looked at him with a hopeful expression.

"Did you find out anything?" she asked.

He was distracted by Rin staring at his back, and he put his arm around Akane's shoulder. She stiffened beneath his touch and tried to pull away, but he held on tight to her.

"Just play along, please."

She looked up at him and maybe there was something pitiful in his expression and that's why she agreed. But feeling the warmth of her body, and her hand pressed against his side brought him comfort.

The temple was nestled at the base of a mountain. It was a small compound lined on all sides. The sloped roofs were hung with ofuda that danced listlessly in the wind. Shin watched it from a distance. It seemed strange that Akio had taken over a temple. There was a strange tint to the place, like a dark shadow hanging over it, even on a bright sunny day. There was an aura that wasn't quite yokai and it wasn't quite human either. He couldn't put his finger on it. It held him back from rushing in.

Shin climbed down from the perch from which he'd been surveying the camp. He and Akane had separated to scout out the area. Shin returned to their designated meeting space, but Akane hadn't returned yet. Even from this distance, he was left with an uneasy feeling twisting in his gut. He didn't like being separated from Akane. Though he'd seen no guards, he got the feeling he was being watched from a distance. He should go and look for her.

He'd only taken a few steps when she appeared around a corner. Shin let go a breath he'd been holding. It struck him, how in such a short time he had become very concerned about her wellbeing. It had taken some convincing to get him to part ways with her, even for a little while. Akio was still out there, he knew, and he wouldn't rest until he had them both.

Akane's brows were furrowed as she strode toward him. Her eyes unseeing. It wasn't like her to be so oblivious to her surroundings.

"Good news?" he asked.

She lifted her head, as if noticing him for the first time. The frown hadn't left her face. "This place has a strange feel to it. It feels tainted."

"I felt that too. It's strange, but I think we can manage," he said with more confidence than he felt. He wasn't sure what Akio was doing with these priestesses, but it wasn't good. All that mattered now though was getting Tomoe and gaining his freedom.

Akane worried at her bottom lip, her gaze on the horizon. "Are you sure? I keep wondering if we shouldn't have asked that kitsune and priest for help."

"No." His voice came out much harsher than he intended.

Akane leveled him with a long stare for a moment and he thought she'd argue. Then she shrugged. "I trust your judgment."

He should have been flattered by the sentiment, but a coil of uncertainty squeezed at his innards. He never used to be the lone wolf. In a past life he'd always worked with others. But centuries as Akio's dog had taught him to rely on himself.

The orange light of a dying day fell behind the mountaintop.

"Let's go then," Shin said with grim determination. Once they had the girl he would be free. And then his hurt pride wouldn't matter.

They headed down the mountain, creeping from behind trees and rocks, getting closer to the temple, keeping an eye out for guards.

The temple was like any other. It contained a main shrine building that should have hosted the kami at its center. Dormitories and storage facilities flanked it on both sides. A low wall surrounded it on all sides. They jumped over it. Once inside, everything was silent. He would have thought the place abandoned if not for the competing scent of priestess and yokai. But mixed among them he caught Tomoe's scent.

"She's here." He signaled to Akane. They snuck between buildings just as a patrol of boar yokai passed by.

They pressed their bodies against the wall, waiting for them to pass before sliding down another passageway toward the dormitory building. Judging from the scent, there were several priestesses inside. This must be the place where they were bringing them all.

The door was locked. Shin tried shaking it and a lock rattled. He froze, waiting to see if it had alerted the guards, but no one came running to stop them.

"We'll have to find another way in." He scanned their surroundings. A few feet away a high window had been left open. "There."

"Give me a leg up?" she asked.

He knelt down and cupped his hands together for her to step in. He hoisted her up, and Akane slithered through the window.

Just as she slipped inside, a shadow moved nearby. Shin pressed his body against the wall. He watched as it moved closer, hoping it would disappear, but it wasn't slowing down. Instead he rushed toward them, hoping to catch them by surprise. But as he turned the corner, he found not a patrolling guard, but the huntsman.

Shin froze. The huntsman did not seem surprised to see him there and instead looked him up and down, leveling him with his gaze.

The huntsman rushed toward him. Shin dodged and rolled, only to have the huntsman's ax graze his side. Shin growled and lunged for him. The huntsman came for him again, and Shin clashed against him, clamping down powerful jaws onto the huntsman's leg. The huntsman shook him off, tossing him across the courtyard. He was outmatched. There was no beating the huntsman, but if he created enough distraction, perhaps Akane and Tomoe could get away.

Shin rose up on shaking feet as the huntsman paced closer to him. But before he could knock Shin down completely, he was thrown backward by a body colliding with him.

Shin shook himself and looked up to see Akane standing there half transformed.

"Tomoe isn't here. It was a trap."

The huntsman tossed Akane aside like she was made of nothing but paper. She slammed into a nearby wall where she crumbled. Shin growled and turned on the huntsman ready to tear his throat out if he must. But the huntsman caught him by the throat and dangled Shin in the air by his collar.

"You cannot disobey Akio. Bring the dragon to him."

The order sparked against the head priestess' bindings on his collar and Shin felt the order reverberate through him, as if it had been issued by Akio himself. It burned up inside him, cowing him back into that sniveling creature who could never disobey Akio. A thin layer of paper was all that remained of the witch's bindings. It was over. Akio had won.

The huntsman dropped him and Shin fell to the ground on all fours. He looked up to see Akane in wolf form standing with her back arched, her eyes glowing red. She lunged for the huntsman, tearing at his throat. He stumbled backward, unable to match the sheer ferocious power of her inner wolf.

She attacked like a wild animal, like a creature lost to all other purposes than killing. Shin transformed into his own wolf form. She'd lost control, but this time it was to their advantage. He stood his ground before her, drawing her attention onto him. She snapped at him, and he growled back, before running for the temple walls. She gave chase, following him as he leaped over the temple walls. He led her on a chase through the forest, and up the mountain with his heart beating wildly in his chest. Every so often he looked back to make sure she still followed and that the huntsman had not.

The pair of wolves ran through the night without stopping. In wolf form they could cross miles at a great speed. It was the one advantage they had against the huntsman. He kept them away from humans, and they did not stop until morning light. He collapsed in an exhausted heap on the ground.

All the fight had gone out of Akane, and she was as a docile as a pup. She was a beautiful wolf. It was a shame she hid this part of her away. Her head rested on her paws as she yawned. Shin curled up next to her and laid his head down, planning to only close his eyes for a moment.

Shin yawned and stretched, working out muscles tight from the previous night's run. It seemed to be midday. Akane was already awake and had resumed her human form. She was staring out at the horizon. He hadn't paid much attention to where they'd gone while they ran. He'd only thought to keep her from losing herself to the bloodlust.

"How did we get here?" she asked, turning toward him.

"We went for a little run," he smiled.

"A little run? We're at the southern seashore." She gestured outward to the sparkling, blue ocean just past the rolling hills.

Without meaning to he'd brought them straight to the dragon's domain. Shin touched the metal collar around his neck. Had Akio's command worked and forced him here? Or had a secret longing of his heart led him here? The bindings still seemed to be intact.

"What do we do now?" Akane asked.

He could see now that turning down Rin's offer of assistance had nearly killed them both. He couldn't do this alone if he wanted to be free and keep Akane safe.

"I think I know someone who can help us."

Seventeen

When Shin had served the dragon, this region had been nothing but forest and beaches. Since then, human villages had popped up all along the coastline. And where a solitary shrine that worshiped the dragon had once stood, a town had risen up around it.

Since the dragon had been freed, Shin had avoided returning. He made a myriad of excuses. But for the same reason he had avoided Rin, it all came down to pride. Shin wasn't the man he'd once been. Now he was nothing but a dog at Akio's disposal. But for Akane, he'd put his pride aside.

There were several entrances to the dragon's palace, but the palace had been abandoned so long many of them were nothing but crumbling ruins. All that remained now was a stone pathway which had emerged from the sea floor and was guarded by a series of red torii arches. It would be invisible to the human eye, as was the palace, which was currently silhouetted by the setting sun. It had taken what was left of that day to get here. The main entryway had been grand at the peak of the dragon's reign.

"Are you sure about this place?" Akane asked as they passed beneath the archways. "It looks abandoned."

She was right, the once mighty fortress walls were crumbling into the sea. The pathway on which they traveled was crusted over with barnacles.

Shin kicked a shell into the ocean along the side of the pathway. "Appearances can be deceiving," he said with a confidence he didn't feel. The dragon had only recently returned after five hundred years sealed in stone. He had a lot of enemies, Akio among them, but he knew his friend. He had a way of instilling hope and loyalty. Before his fall, he'd been the most powerful being in Akatsuki. If anyone could help him save Tomoe, it was him.

Akane took a few steps before realizing he'd stopped walking and turned to face him. "Who is this friend of yours?"

"The dragon, the ruler of Akatsuki," Shin said with a wave of his hand.

"The Dragon. The same dragon who destroyed the armies of the eight, and rose to power in bloodshed?" She asked, her mouth hanging open.

What would she think if she found out he was there fighting beside the dragon as he struggled for control over Akatsuki? Now wasn't the time to reveal that particular fact. She'd just started to trust him. He'd tell her about it later. That was if there was a later for them. He hadn't thought much about what happened once he was free of Akio. Surely once they saved Tomoe she'd return to her shrine and he'd... his gaze drifted toward the palace walls. The empty shadow of his once worthy past. Could he return to this place?

He'd almost forgotten about those days, standing by the dragon's side as a general over legions of yokai. What was he now but Akio's dog to be kicked around? He balled his hand into a fist. Not anymore. He would be free soon, and return to the formidable yokai he had been.

"He's not like the stories." He resumed a brisk walk toward the main gate.

Akane followed, but he could feel her reluctance as she lagged behind. They approached the gates of the palace, and he planned on walking right in. He'd done so the last time he'd come here on Akio's orders. Shortly after the dragon had returned, Akio had sent him here to taunt the dragon and remind him and Shin who was in control. He pushed the memory away.

As they got close to the gates however, two hulking oni stepped out from behind the walls.

"Who are you, and what is your purpose here?" one asked in a rumbling voice.

"I could ask the same. I don't remember the dragon having oni guards." Shin eyed them up and down.

"Speak," the oni growled. Typically, they were dumb creatures and easily distracted and confused. These two were not like others he'd met.

Shin stepped toward them, palms up in a supplicant gesture. "I'm here to see the dragon."

"No one sees the dragon," the oni grumbled and took a step toward Shin brandishing his weapon.

Maybe he'd given him too much credit. Akane, seeing a threat, had sprung into action and fired a volley of arrows at the oni. And then the oni's friend, seeing they were under attack, charged them as well. The ground shook beneath their feet as the massive yokai came thundering toward them. Akane's arrows bounced ineffectually off their leathery skin.

"Akane do—" Before he could finish his sentence, the oni who was closest to him swung, and Shin, being closest to him, was knocked off his feet and sent careening into the ocean.

The shock of cold water forced the air out of his lungs. He gasped as his lungs filled with water. Normally drowning wasn't a concern for a yokai - it took more than some ingested water. But it wasn't just oni guarding the palace. While swimming up to the surface, a tentacle wrapped around his ankle and pulled him down fast. As he sank into the depths, the light on the surface faded to a mere pinprick. He kicked and flailed to no avail.

Bubbles were expelled from his throat as his lungs made a feeble attempt to inhale. Shin's outstretched hand reached upward toward the sky he could no longer see. Darkness crept into the edges of his vision, and his eyes drooped. He tried to fight it, but all the energy was being drained from him. What a pathetic end. He'd been so close to freedom and this is how he died?

A hand grasped around his wrist and yanked him upward. Caught in a strange tug of war between whatever was yanking him downward and what was pulling him up, he peered through the gloom to see Akane's face twisted in concentration. She removed a hidden dagger from her waist and slashed at the tentacle wrapped around his ankle. The creature screeched, the vibrations slamming into him. It reeled backward, and while it was distracted, Akane wrapped her arm around his waist and pulled him toward the surface. Once he was above water again, he sputtered and coughed out the liquid filling his lungs.

"That's twice you saved my life now," Shin gasped as they bobbed on the ocean's surface.

Along the pathway where they'd fallen from, a small group gathered. They were outnumbered. Not that he wanted to fight them. But Akane hadn't exactly made a good first impression. From behind the crowd, an unfamiliar dragon pushed forward.

"Don't fight them," Shin instructed Akane. "I'll explain everything."

The yokai pointed their weapons at him as he swam closer.

"Stand back," said the dragon at the head of the group.

"My name is Shin. I'm a friend of the dragon. Let him I know I've come looking for help, he'll let us in."

The dragon frowned and looked back at the palace. A woman came running toward the crowd on the path. Her hands danced with flames. He was surprised to see it was a woman he knew. But not from the old days. He'd run into her on a mission for Akio. It hadn't been a friendly encounter. He never thought he'd see a human in the dragon's palace. Things must have changed. This must be the woman the dragon had been rumored to be traveling with.

"What happened?" She asked the dragon, who seemed to be the leader here.

The dragon ran a hand through her maroon hair, avoiding looking at the priestess. She scowled at the dragon before her gaze fell on Shin and Akane.

"You!" She pointed at him.

"Funny running into you here," he said with a grin.

"What are you doing here?" she asked. She hadn't lowered her flaming hands, which he could understand since the last time they had run into one another they were trying to kill one another.

"I could ask the same of you."

"Are you trying to get us killed?" Akane hissed from his side.

She was right. If this were the dragon's lover, he would need to get on her good side. From what he'd seen of her thus far, she had quite the temper.

"I'm here to see the dragon," Shin replied to her original question.

"You work for the horrid pig, don't you? What does he want with Kaito?" She scanned him up and down. She clearly didn't trust him.

Before he could explain himself, a familiar voice said, "What is going on here?"

The assembled yokai all turned and bowed deeply, everyone except for the priestess who continued to stand nearby with narrowed eyes on Shin and Akane. The dragon marched in, his hair tied up in a top knot and wearing gleaming, silver armor. It was like stepping back into the past, to the days when they weren't sure they'd see the next sunrise. The dragon truly had returned.

The dragon scanned over the crowd then to Shin and Akane, who were still treading water a few feet away.

"What are you doing?" The dragon looked torn between amusement and confusion.

"Just going for a swim," Shin said with a shrug or at least the best he could manage while treading water.

The dragon went to the edge of the path, extending a hand to help Shin out. Once he pulled Shin up, he wrapped him into a fierce embrace. When they broke away, Shin turned to help Akane out of the water. She and the priestess were staring one another up and down.

"You know him?" the priestess asked, nodding toward Shin with disapproval.

"Shin is my old friend and general," the dragon said as he slung his arm over Shin's shoulder.

Then the dragon looked between Shin and the priestess with narrowed eyes. "You've met before? Why have I not heard about this?"

"It's a long story," Shin said with a laugh. "Right?" he asked the priestess.

She rolled her eyes. "You could say that."

The dragon tightened his grip on Shin. "That's a story I'd want to hear."

Shin grinned. The dragon hadn't changed at all. This must be his woman. The pair of them had always been rivals as much as friends, including when it came to women. He chuckled to himself, thinking of how they'd fallen over themselves trying to woo ladies of the dragon's court.

"I'd be happy to tell it. But first, I have important matters to speak with you about."

The dragon's expression turned from joy to suspicion. "I was hoping you'd escaped Akio at last."

Shin shook his head and then the dragon's gaze fell on Akane who was still gripping her bow like a lifeline.

The dragon nodded and gestured for Shin to follow him. They passed through a courtyard that bustled with activity, yokai around them carried weapons and building materials. As they traveled down a twisting hallway that was both familiar and foreign, the sounds of repairs echoed around them. He led them into a chamber which was dominated by a massive map of Akatsuki. It had to have been intentional. How many days had they spent pouring over this map together, planning some strategy or another.

The dragon smiled at him, sharing unspoken memories. Then his smile fell as he leaned against the map table. This was the face of a ruler, hard and merciless. They might have been friends, but his kingdom came first.

"How can I help you and..." He looked at Akane with a quirked brow.

"This is Akane."

She was standing very still, her eyes scanning the room rapidly.

The dragon quirked an eyebrow in Shin's direction. As if to say: and who is she to you...? Shin shook his head in reply. Now was not the time for talk of conquests, which is surely what the dragon saw her as. The very idea filled him with irrational rage.

"We are here to ask you for your help," Shin said, trying to get to the point.

"We?" A smirk played at the corner of the dragon's lips as he looked between them suggestively.

"It's not like that." Shin sighed in exasperation, while Akane's face had turned a bright crimson.

"That's not what Rin tells me. She said she met you two at an inn?"

"Shin and I have been working together to find a priestess, a kamigakari candidate. Akio has her and we need your help to rescue her."

The dragon's mischievous smile fell. And then his eyes fell to the collar around Shin's neck. Shin touched his collar.

"I see. Well I'm afraid I'm busy with my own troubles at the moment." He paced around the table. "I was hoping when you came back you'd be ready to join me again."

Akane was staring between the two of them. "How do you know one another?"

"Shin was my general, until Akio stole him away from me."

"Then if you want him back, you should help us. My head priestess can break Akio's hold over him, but only if he brings back Tomoe."

The dragon's dark gaze flicked toward Akane, studying her for the moment. Then he went back to Shin.

"I would like to help, really, I would, but right now I'm being threatened on two fronts. The humans and other yokai are rising up against me. I can't just go looking for some girl. Even for you, my old friend."

"If not you, can you spare any of your men?" Akane pleaded.

The dragon sighed. "There aren't many I could spare. Unless Rin—"

"No," Shin said, cutting off the thought before it was uttered.

The dragon looked at him, his expression softening. He knew the history that kept him back.

"Why not? She helped us find that temple, maybe she could help us again?" Akane said.

"We'll find another way," Shin said, trying to cut her off.

"What is it about her? Why are you so afraid of taking her help?"

"I'm the reason he's been Akio's slave for five hundred years." Shin turned to the door where Rin stood. A part of him knew by coming here he'd run the risk of running into her again. But it seemed there was no avoiding it now.

The dragon came and placed a hand on Akane's shoulder. "I think we should let them talk."

Shin was glad to see Akane shake off his touch. She glanced once more back at him before following the dragon out the door, leaving Rin and him alone.

EIGHTEEN

The distance between them was a giant chasm. Though he wanted to run from the room, and from this palace, he was frozen in place. Rin's gaze pierced him. It held him captive and wouldn't let him go. No one knew him better than her. Before a thought was uttered she was ready with a response.

"Did you lure me here just to ambush me?" The bitter words spilled from his lips before he could stop them. Though he kept on running from her, Rin kept on chasing him.

"It's not an ambush. We're friends, aren't we?"

But that had been before he'd served Akio. Shin was haunted by what he had done. He'd killed friends at Akio's command. He'd tortured the innocent, lied and cheated. All for Akio's twisted amusement. How could he face her knowing what he had done?

Without Rin's customary smile, her face looked pinched and muted. Coward that he was, he couldn't face her. His eyes scanned the old, familiar map, enchanted to change as the landscape did. Human settlements and farms scarred the landscape where once before had been nothing but wild country. At the center—the sprawling palace of the emperor.

"Can you at least look at me?" Rin said. Her voice caught.

Shin gripped the edge of the map table, his nails digging into the wood. "I'd rather not if you don't mind."

Her footsteps padded on the floor behind him. He felt each inch she moved closer: that achingly familiar scent, the even cadence of her heartbeat, and her spiritual aura which shined like the brightest day in his mind's eye. He'd never been a stranger to death. As the dragon's general, he was often needed to defend his rule, or take out his enemies. Though it had been his choice to serve his friend, it wasn't easy. Rin helped him heal, she chased away the dark thoughts. Many women had walked in and out of his life. No one could ever replace the space Rin took up in his heart.

Until he forced her out. He'd spent five hundred years trying to forget her. Failing to forget her. Because she kept on coming back. He didn't want to bring her into Akio's world. He couldn't stand her getting wrapped up in his twisted games.

She put her hand on his shoulder. For a moment he indulged in her touch, but it held none of the comfort it had before. Perhaps he'd grown jaded, dead on the inside. Maybe he would have continued down that path had it not been for Akane. She awoke compassion in him again, she made him believe he wasn't entirely wicked.

He stepped out of Rin's embrace. Spinning around, he leaned against the table's edge, arms crossed over his chest. He kept his gaze stubbornly off of Rin, and instead his eyes tracked over the tendrils of black mold creeping over the far wall.

"I want to help you break free." She tilted her head, trying to catch his eye. But he only twisted his neck further to avoid her gaze.

"No thanks."

"Damn it, Shin. Don't keep blocking me out." She stamped her foot on the floor. She so rarely lost her temper, he'd never pushed her this far before.

"I think we're done here." He couldn't stand it. He had to run before he made an even bigger fool of himself. He brushed past her and headed for the door.

Before he could get very far, she grabbed onto his wrist, stopping him in his tracks.

"Please. Stop running away from me." Emotion made her voice thick.

He never wanted to make Rin cry. She knew he was a sucker for her tears.

Shin let go a ragged breath. "We can't go back to who we were."

"Don't be ridiculous."

He pulled away and made for the door.

"I've been looking into the missing girls. I know where Akio has taken them."

He stopped. The seconds ticked by as he debated.

"You were confident last time as well."

"I didn't know it would be a trap. Hikaru has scouted the location himself. This time it's for real."

"Tell me where it is," he said, keeping his back to her. If he faced her he was afraid his last shred of pride would crumble.

"Not unless you promise to rejoin the dragon."

Shin spun in anger, raising his hand as if he would strike her. Not that he ever would, but he wanted her to think that. For her to see what a monster he'd become and forget about him. Rin's gaze was steady. She didn't even flinch as his hand came inches from her face.

"You act like I don't know you, Shin," she said, the ghost of a smile on her lips.

"I'm not who I was."

"That's what you say."

He growled and paced away from her. He stalked around the table, putting it between them. As if distance would make any difference.

"It was always easier for you. To smile and pretend everything was alright." He tightened his hand into a fist.

"We can't go back to who we were, but we can move forward as who we are now." Her eyes were beseeching.

"You don't know what I've done. The atrocities I've committed."

"That wasn't your choice. How could I condemn you when you're there because of me?"

Shin raised his head, meeting her gaze. And it was then he realized. It had never been about what he'd done. Rin forgave him, even as he hurt her over and over again. It was because he wanted her to suffer as he had. Because somewhere along the way, his love for her had transformed into hatred.

He leaned forward onto the table. He felt as if the wind had been knocked out of him. "What have I done?"

Rin came around the table and pressed her hand onto his shoulder. She said nothing but the weight of her hand was a comfort. He sighed. Once upon a time being close to her had filled him with a desperate longing. Perhaps he'd placed her just out of reach because he knew he could never have her. Because even before Hikaru, he had liked things as they were and didn't want to complicate it with romance. Though he wanted to go back to that, he didn't think it was possible. Once more he thought of Akane, as she laid beside him while the poison ravaged his body. Even Rin hadn't seen him at his most vulnerable.

He didn't love Rin anymore, not like he had. But he didn't hate her either. He just felt numb.

Rin took a step back and with a bright smile she bowed and said, "My name is Rin, nice to meet you."

He shook his head. "What are you doing?"

"And your name?" she gestured with her hand for him to introduce himself.

He smirked before bowing in return. "Shin."

When he stood up again, Rin was watching him with that mischievous look in her eyes. "We're starting over you and me. The past is behind us, and this is a new day."

"Were you always this insufferably positive?"

"How would you know? We just met."

Shin laughed long and hard. Rin joined him, laughing along with him until their sides hurt. Once they'd composed themselves they headed for the door. As they exited, his eyes searched out Akane. She and the dragon hadn't gone far. The dragon was in a heated debate with the flame priestess. Akane stood a few feet from them and had her hand within reach of her bow and her eyes scanning the hallway. Their eyes met, and he felt a flutter in his chest when she smiled at him.

It would seem he hadn't learned his lesson when it came to falling for women who he couldn't have.

THE FLAME PRIESTESS AND THE DRAGON WERE ARGUING AGAIN. Her hands sparked and she gestured with her hands. The dragon had a smirk on his lips, like he found her frustration amusing. It was never clear what their disputes were about. Akane had been at the dragon's palace for less than a day and she'd seen them squabble at least a half dozen times since she'd arrived.

Shin was busy making plans for their rescue of Tomoe. Akane had needed some air. Being around this many yokai made her inner wolf rise closer to the surface. Her senses were heightened and the smell of all the yokai was over-whelming. She'd snuck off to this far-flung, abandoned courtyard hoping to get some peace and quiet. And instead stumbled upon this pair.

Well, rather, they'd come to where she was hiding behind a half-crumbled wall, her face toward the ocean. She thought about interrupting, but by the time she'd gotten up the courage, they were well into their argument, and she figured it better to just wait them out.

"You think I can't do it?" the flame priestess argued.

"You'd be walking right into danger. I think it's a stupid plan."

"So, I'm stupid?"

Akane sighed. Why didn't they just kiss and get it over with already? They clearly were attracted to one another. She'd spotted both of them watching each other, always when the other was looking away. She thought it strange to find a priestess in their midst. But she wasn't the only one. Akane had met several other priests here in the palace. She hadn't thought humans and yokai could co-exist. What would Mei have thought if she'd lived to see it?

"You're wanted in the map room," Shin said, interrupting their argument.

Akane peaked around the crumbled wall and saw the flame priestess with her arms crossed over her chest.

"We'll finish this discussion later," the dragon said before storming away.

To his retreating back she said, "There's nothing left to say!"

Akane listened to their retreating footsteps before removing herself from her hiding spot. She'd have to remember to avoid this place in the future. Not that there was a future for her here. Once she had Tomoe, she'd go back to the palace. And that would mean saying goodbye to Shin as well. The thought caught like a lump in her throat.

"Do you think they're lovers?" Shin asked from behind her. His breath tickled the back of her neck, making the hairs stand on end. She hadn't noticed him hiding in the shadows waiting for her to emerge.

She jumped and spun around to chastise him, only to realize he was dangerously close. Akane stared at his throat, the musky scent of wolf was wafting off him like a forbidden temptation. Reluctantly, she lifted her gaze to meet his golden eyes, which were crinkled in amusement.

She cleared her throat and stepped away from him. "How did you know I was here?"

He chuckled under his breath. It felt intimate and dangerous. The wolf within her wanted him, that was the only way to explain these feelings. And with it so close to the surface it was overriding her more rational feelings. Akane pressed her hand against her beating heart, willing her nerves to calm.

"I came looking for you. The dragon wasn't really needed in the map room," he said.

"Ah." She cleared her throat. She felt suddenly awkward as if he could read her attraction on her face.

"I thought you might be a little overwhelmed by all the yokai. You can stay here if you need more time, I'll keep guard."

She stared at him wide-eyed. How had he known what she needed without her telling him? She swallowed past a lump in her throat.

"Thank you." She turned and considered going back to her hiding spot, but at the last second changed her mind.

"Actually, I'm feeling a lot better. If you wanted to stay here with me?"

He smiled. "I'd like that."

NINETEEN

They arrived at their destination on a moonless night, perfect for a sneak attack. Shin, Akane, Rin and Hikaru would all be going into the temple from different directions.

Akane gripped her bow tight in her hand, counting down the seconds in her mind. From her vantage point she couldn't see much of the temple, but the stench of the acidic tang of corruption hung on the air. It commingled with the spicy scent of fear. Unlike the first temple, this one was clearly filled with priestesses. Apart from the scents, there were yokai guarding on all corners. She should have known the first temple was a trap. But tonight, she would save Tomoe.

A bird called out in the night. It was Hikaru's signal. Using the darkness to cloak her, Akane snuck up to the walls which surrounded the temple. Her heart slammed against her rib cage, threatening to burst from her chest. Her inner wolf paced restlessly within her. The sensation of danger on the air had the hairs on the back of her neck standing on end. Akane's overlong claws scraped the plaster wall as she sailed over it.

A howl pierced the night, echoed by the roar of yokai. Shin. Akane froze, listening as the clash of weapons faded into the night. She cocked her head toward the sound, straining to hear. The wind whistled between the buildings and sent a cold chill down her back. Her inner wolf growled, pulling taut at her leash. She wanted to protect Shin. But Tomoe needed her. They'd made a plan. Akane was to find Tomoe and get her out. The others would distract Akio's guards.

A small gap between buildings made for convenient cover. Akane squeezed between buildings, her quiver scraping against the wall. Temples were meant to be holy places, home of the kami. They were supposed to be pure. This place was the reverse. It felt slimy, corrupt, and being inside it felt like walking through mud. The sooner she got out of here, the better.

Across a moonlight courtyard was another dormitory building. It was shrouded in darkness, not even a single candle was lit within. The wind turned in her direction and carried the scent of human with it. Tomoe had to be there. Akane looked both ways before darting out from cover. She was cut short when a yokai stepped out of the shadows and blocked her way.

She drew her bow. But this thing - it wasn't a yokai. But it wasn't human either. The monster had horns curling and bursting from its skull, where the skin still bled as if it was from a fresh wound. The legs were uneven and it moved with a waddling gait. The body was massive, with one arm too small. In the human-sized hand it carried an ofuda, a blessed piece of paper, a tool of those that served the kami.

But a monster like this should not be able to wield it. Akane's hands were on the bow, pulling back and prepared to loose her arrow and impale it. But then she saw the monster look at her and it was the face of a human woman. Tomoe.

Akane froze as the monster lumbered closer. It sang an incantation and threw the ofuda toward her. It couldn't be Tomoe. Her eyes were closer together and her nose was too big. But what had created such an abomination?

Blue flames engulfed the ofuda seconds before it collided with Akane.

"You keep going," Rin roared as she placed herself between Akane and the monster.

Akane shook her head. Whatever those monsters were, she didn't want to know. She blundered forward toward the dormitory building. A blood-curdling scream came from within it. Akane tried the door, but it was locked. Without time to waste, she kicked it in. Shards of wood went flying as she rushed inside.

Half a dozen girls were bent over, screaming as they clasped their heads. A woman in all black, her face obscured by a hood, sang a strange song full of notes of discord mixed with high lilting tunes. The sound rang inside Akane's skull, bringing her to her knees as well. The priestesses clawed at their skulls, their faces contorted in pain. And then one girl stood up, her back arched. Her skin burst apart with a wet, ripping sound. Scales emerged from beneath the torn flesh, and spikes jutted out of her back. Then a second and third girl suffered the same fate, transforming them all into monstrosities like what she'd seen in the courtyard.

The song dug into Akane's ears. She slammed her hands over her them, trying to block it out. But it was no use, Akane fell to her knees as a burning pain raced across her body. Her blood thrummed in her ears, and the scent of fire and blood were thick on the air. All around her were sights and sounds almost too overwhelming to process. But then from the corner of her eye, she saw one of the monsters created by the song stumble toward her.

Her transformation was quick and hard. As a wolf she attacked, going for its throat, tearing it out and filling her mouth with a vile, bitter taste. She leaped back, watching a mixture of black and red blood swirl together and pool on the ground, thick as oil. She got closer and sniffed before blowing out the repugnant scent.

The remaining monsters closed in around her, dripping blood from where their flesh had been ripped open. The hairs on her back bristled as she growled at them in warning. They sang in reply, the notes tainted with dissonance and it made her skin crawl as the power attempted to subdue her. It froze her in place. The monster's song was too powerful. They closed in around her, close enough that she could see the whites of their bloodshot eyes.

One of them reached for her, but as they did she put all her energy into breaking their spell. With powerful front paws, she knocked the nearest creature to the ground and tore into its tainted flesh. Another came up behind her, trying to sing her into submission, but Akane turned and clawed at their abdomen. Black and red blood poured from the wound. The murderous rampage went on in a blur, until she was left panting and splattered with ichor and blood.

The battle for the temple raged around her. The stench of those monsters was everywhere. Akane scented the air and there were more of the abominations nearby. She took a step in their direction but as she did, she caught Tomoe's scent. She followed it to the main shrine building where the kami should be housed.

In wolf form she couldn't open the door but with a few kicks of powerful paws, she knocked it down. Once she was inside the room, tainted energy hit her like a slap to the face. The holy place had been defiled. The sacred icons were missing, and resting on a pedestal were small round stones. A priest with black tattoos on his face held one of the black orbs over a trembling girl, who was being held in place by two other priests.

It was all a perverse version of the kamigakari ceremony. The ghosts of old memories came up from the deepest recesses of her mind. A woman screamed her name, begging her to stop. There were fire and blood. The wolf pushed these sympathetic thoughts away. She had one job, save Tomoe. The priests turned as she entered, but their song rolled off her ineffectually. She tore them down with claws and teeth, leaving their broken bodies behind, their crimson blood staining the tatami. Tomoe had her back pressed against the wall, and grasped a candle stand, swinging it in front of her.

"Don't come any closer," she said, her voice shaking.

Very slowly Akane approached her. She'd never shown this form to Tomoe. She hadn't dared since she'd killed Mei. But it felt like she was waking up from a long dream. She hadn't realized it while she was fighting those horrid creatures, but she hadn't lost control of her sense of self. Or her duty to save Tomoe. How could that be possible? She could smell the stench of corruption on Tomoe, but it was just a thin veneer, like a scum on the surface of a pond.

She pressed her nose against Tomoe's elbow, nudging her gently. The scent of taint made her nose flutter. She stepped back just in case she lost control and tried to hurt Tomoe. But the kami's justice did not overtake her. Akane was still sane. She was herself.

"Tomoe, it's me, Akane," Akane said.

Very slowly, Tomoe reached out to place her hand against Akane's cheek. Her fingers tangled in her white fur.

"Akane, is that really you?" Her voice was hoarse and cracked.

Akane nodded.

Tomoe rushed forward, wrapping her arms around the scruff of Akane's neck. She'd done it. She'd controlled her wolf. And more importantly, she'd saved Tomoe.

Twenty

The audience hall was bursting with yokai. Shin weaved his way through the crowd. Music and laughter, lubricated by too much sake, drifted toward the ceiling. Kegs of the liquor had been brought out from the old stores and everyone was happy and full of life. It felt like the old days again.

Every few feet, someone would stop and slap him on the back. They all recognized him now. The dragon's oldest friend and his former general. That felt like the old days too. Everyone that wanted to get closer to the dragon tried to use Shin to do so. Women who hoped to draw the dragon's attention would flirt with Shin first, knowing of their rivalry. Men who wanted a favor plied Shin with gifts, hoping he'd get the dragon's ear. Back then he hadn't minded. The dragon and he had laughed about it often.

Right now, all he wanted to do was talk to Akane. She hated crowds, he knew. Since they'd rescued Tomoe, everything had been a blur. They'd escaped with Tomoe, but he'd delayed returning her to her temple by saying he needed time to recover from his injuries.

As he made his way through the crowd, he saw the dragon and the human priestess in another argument from across the room. Shin shook his head. Their bickering was legendary, apparently. It seemed strange the dragon would be attracted to a woman like that. And yet, Shin had seen the way he'd looked at her when she wasn't looking, with adoration in his gaze. In all their years of friendship, he'd never seen the dragon look at someone that way.

Shin turned away from his friend and his love troubles to resume his search for Akane. He found her on the edge of the room, her arms over her chest and her head bobbing back and forth as she scanned the crowd. Was she looking for him? It might have been arrogant to hope so. As he snuck up behind her, she muttered something under her breath he couldn't quite make out.

He put his hands on her waist and she almost leaped five feet in the air. She spun around to face him, teeth bared as if she'd tear his throat out. But when she saw him, her expression relaxed. And dare he hope, she looked happy to see him.

"You scared me to death," she said as she pulled away and clutched her throat.

"You've been avoiding me ever since we got back."

She crossed her arms over her chest and refused to look at him directly. "I wasn't avoiding you, I was busy making sure Tomoe was okay. I've lost her again... There's a lot of yokai here and she just went through a terrible ordeal..." she trailed off, her gaze meeting his. "Why are you smiling?"

He hadn't even realized his amusement was showing on his face. He coughed to cover it up. "No reason," he said, trying to look away from her to spare her further embarrassment. How had he never noticed how adorable she was when she was making excuses? In fact, there were many qualities he'd come to admire in her during their time together.

They both stood in strained silence for a moment before Akane said, "Thank you."

Shin blinked a few times, staring at her in confusion. "For what?"

She rubbed her arm with her palm. "For helping me find Tomoe," she mumbled under her breath.

Shin smiled and leaned in closer to her. Her clean scent taunted his nostrils. "I'm sorry. I couldn't quite hear that," he breathed.

"For—" She whipped her head around to meet his gaze, and suddenly they were inches apart. Her breath caught and he could feel his pulse throbbing in his throat. The noise of the room around them had dimmed and it was if they were the only two people in the entire world.

Akane parted her lips slightly. "I—" she stuttered.

"You?"

She swallowed hard and turned away from him, shattering the moment into a million pieces. He cleared his throat and straightened up. Of course she didn't see him that way, not that it mattered. They couldn't be together for a thousand different reasons. If she were any other women he would have considered a one-time fling, but he knew one night with her would never be enough.

"I should go find Tomoe," Akane said, gesturing to the crowded room. Though he'd come to expect her avoidance, it still disappointed him. She took a few steps and turned around to say, "If you want, maybe we can talk later?"

Shin grinned. "I'd like that."

She blushed and spun away from him. One little word, 'later.' It was filled with promise and expectation. Could there be more? The very idea sent his heart racing. His eyes followed her as she wended through the crowd toward Tomoe, who was flirting with a handsome yokai that Shin didn't recognize.

"You're in a good mood."

Shin turned and Rin smiled at him mischievously. Before her smile rivaled the sun, and he had always turned toward it for warmth. But it wasn't the same. That same feeling he'd been chasing for so long had dimmed.

"It's a time for celebration, why wouldn't I be?" he said as he ran his hands through his hair.

"You're really taken by her, aren't you?" she asked and brought his attention back to her. There was a mischievous glint in Rin's eye. There was probably no one that knew him better than her. It shouldn't have come at a surprise that she'd figured it out. For centuries he had thought himself in love with her. He had given up everything to protect her, so it felt wrong to talk about another woman with her, like he was betraying her somehow.

"I've heard the dragon has made you into a general," Shin said to change the subject. "You've risen high. You're no longer his messenger."

She narrowed her eyes at him. "Trying to change the subject? Fine. What about *you?* I heard he wants you to take up your old position."

The dragon hadn't asked him formally, not yet. But the question was coming, he knew it. And, of course, that would be the logical next step. But he was hesitating. Not because of any lingering resentment to Rin or even the dragon. But because of well... Shin tugged at his collar. "Nothing is decided yet."

Rin stared at the collar around his neck, her expression falling. "Five hundred years," she muttered to herself.

Five hundred years of servitude, of torture, or pain. At times he had cursed himself for making that choice, but he wouldn't have met Akane if he hadn't.

"I would do it again, given the choice," he said to assure her. And he meant it.

Rin's eyes flickered up to him and tears were welling along her lashes. She threw her arms around his neck, squeezing him tight.

She leaned in, whispering in his ear, "You've done enough. You can be happy now."

He froze in her arms. At one time they had been each other's comfort, the only ones in this world that mattered. He loved her, and always would. But it was never meant to be. He'd held onto his love for her, and like a token it had kept him sane in that terrible place. But he was nearly free and it was time to move on from the past. Shin stepped back and looked in her eyes.

"I never deserved you."

She smiled up at him. "I don't deserve you."

He leaned forward and planted a kiss on her forehead. It was goodbye: to the people they'd been, to what he'd always hoped for. They broke apart and as he turned he spotted Akane. She stared at them, eyes wide. He could only imagine how this must look to her.

He took a step toward her but before he could reach her, she turned on her feet and ran the other direction, disappearing into the crowd.

"Akane!" He shouted her name and tried to chase after her, but before he could get very far another crowd of yokai got in the way. When he broke free of them at last, he'd lost sight of her. He ran for the hall and turned in a circle, but she was gone. He growled in frustration.

A hand came down hard on his shoulder. He turned around to see the dragon smiling at him.

"Come, drink with me." It was said more like a command than a request. But Shin was in no mood for cavorting. He had to explain himself to Akane.

"Not now," Shin said as he shook himself loose of his friend.

The dragon ran in front of him, blocking his path. "I have something to talk to you about," the dragon said.

"We'll talk later," Shin replied, attempting to dodge.

He wasn't quick enough and the dragon caught him in a headlock. Shin struggled against him as the dragon said, "You're not disappearing on me again."

"Fine, what is it?" Shin snarled.

"I want you to bear my child," the dragon teased.

Shin pulled himself out of the headlock and took a playful swing at him. "You really have the worst timing."

"Women troubles?" The dragon smirked knowingly. "You dog, you haven't changed at all."

This type of teasing was normal for them. But this time he'd hit too close to the mark. What had Akane heard about him since they'd been back at the palace? Had she heard about his womanizing past and come to the wrong conclusion?

"I'm in no mood for you." Shin pushed past him and ran in the direction Akane had gone. The dragon shouted after him. Shin ignored him.

Drunk yokai wandered the halls, and he could just imagine how upset she would be to be surrounded by them. She still wasn't comfortable around her own kind. After searching for what felt like forever, he found her alone in a deserted garden. She had her head tilted back, staring at the sliver of moon in the sky. As he approached, he froze. Entranced by her and terrified to cross that distance. There had been hundreds of women over the centuries, and he'd always kept them at a distance. It was easier. Feelings were messy. If he opened himself up to her and she rejected him, he wasn't sure he could take it. She must have sensed him, because she turned toward him with wide eyes brimming with tears. When she realized it was him, she turned and tried to disguise them by rubbing them away.

"I'm not really in the mood to talk." Her voice was like a knife to the heart.

"Rin is just a friend."

She turned to him with a watery smile. "You don't have to explain. I know she's the reason you sold yourself to Akio. I'm happy for you both, really."

The words sounded so final to him. As if she'd slammed the door in his face. Maybe it would be better to walk away, with minimal heartache. The potential for more was different than the real thing. She didn't feel welcome here, and this was where he belonged.

Akane attempted to brush past him. "I have to go find Tomoe."

Shin grabbed her by the wrist. A small frown pulled her brows together. He'd hesitated with Rin, he wasn't going to do the same with Akane.

"I loved Rin."

She turned away from him. "You're back where you belong then."

"I don't love her anymore, not in the way I used to. She'll always have a place in my heart. But there's someone else who occupies that space now."

She was very still, like a rabbit in his sights. As if he made one wrong move, she would bolt.

"Who?" Her voice was husky.

Very gently, he turned her to face him, his hands resting on her arms. She didn't back away this time. Her eyes were darting across his face.

"Well, that depends on you."

She swallowed hard. "What does that mean?"

When he wanted, he could be charming. But standing here, his raw emotions laid out for her, there was only one way he could think to say how he felt. He pulled her closer. With his hands on her back, her thundering heart against his chest, he kissed her.

TWENTY-ONE

Shin was a very good kisser. All her doubts faded away when he wrapped his arms around her. It felt right. His tongue parted her lips, exploring her mouth, and his hands tangled in her hair. Their chests were pressed together, their hearts beating in time with one another. And then much too soon, they broke apart, and Shin took a step back. His golden eyes scanned hers.

"I shouldn't have done that." It was the first time she'd seem him seem unsure. It was endearing. But he'd awoken a hunger in her. A warm, glowing need was coiling in her belly.

Her inner wolf howled, desperate for his touch. Forming words was beyond her. It felt as if she was being consumed by her desire. But she and her inner wolf were no longer two minds sharing a body. From that night she'd fallen asleep curled up next to him, to all the little moments in between, it had all been leading up this. Her wolf had sensed it. They were of one mind and they both wanted Shin. No one else could calm her at her most wild. She'd tried to deny it, but there were no more excuses left. She grabbed hold of his kosode. She bunched the cloth in her fist, bringing him closer, smashing her mouth against his. Teeth brushed against each other in her urgency to feel his tongue swipe against her lips. His hands roved over her body, caressing the swell of her hips, and curve of her rear, which he squeezed. She ground her groin against him as she clawed her nails across his back, ripping the fabric in her need.

He walked her backward, pushing her back against a nearby wall. His palm, smooth against her belly, hitched up her haori. Her breath caught.

Laughter floated down the hallway. They broke apart, panting as the yokai passed by. She devoured him with her eyes as he watched the intruders walk on past.

"Perhaps we should go somewhere more private."

"I think that would be best," she said a little breathless.

He grabbed her hand and led her down the hall. Her pulse was dancing, her entire body burning with need. After a brief search, they found an empty room. As soon as the door closed behind them, Akane leaped onto Shin, wrapping her legs around his hips. He nuzzled against her neck, his tongue flicking against her sensitive skin. Akane groaned. Shin laid her down on the futon, leaning above her. His eyes trailed over her face, then down. Akane arched her back as she slipped out of her haori. Her exposed flesh pebbled in the cool night air. Shin kissed down her chest to her bellybutton. Then he looked up at her.

"If you want we can stop," he said.

Her breath was heavy and the scent of him intoxicating. All she could think about was him. How she needed him, to really feel whole. To mend that last broken piece of her heart.

"I don't want to stop." She pulled him back up toward her, kissing him again.

AKANE WOKE THE NEXT MORNING, HER BODY LANGUID AND loose. Shin's arm wrapped around her waist and held her close. It was like the night she'd woken up in the forest with him tangled around her but different. So much different. Thinking about the night before, a blush stained her cheeks. Being with Shin was like nothing she'd experienced before. She felt complete. Shin stirred against her and pressed himself to her backside.

"Ready for round two?" he purred in her ear.

Akane smiled and spun around to face him. Kissing him gently, she said against his lips, "I thought you would be tired after last night."

"You think that's all I have in me?" He smiled against her.

But their kiss was cut short when the door flew open and Tomoe stormed in. "Akane we need to talk—" She froze mid-sentence, eyes wide.

Akane jumped up and covered herself with the blanket while Shin did the same.

Tomoe's eyes darted from Shin to Akane, then a slow smile spread over her lips. "You two? Did you?"

Akane grabbed Shin's clothes off the ground and tossed them at him, before wrapping the blanket around herself and ushering Tomoe out the door. Tomoe attempted to peak her head over her shoulder to catch a glimpse of a naked Shin, presumably, but Akane had her out of the room before she had the chance.

She exhaled and leaned against the door. Shin had put on his hakama, but his bare chest was exposed, and the trail of hair that led downward caught her gaze for a moment. He smirked at her assessment. He strolled over and planted his arms on either side of the door and planted a kiss on Akane's lips. She melted all over again. If she had the chance, she'd join him for another roll in the futon.

But Tomoe banged on the door. "You can't keep me out here forever!"

Akane sighed.

"I probably should let you handle that." He stepped back and Akane ached for him. There was so much more she wanted to do with him before she returned to the temple. It struck her then just how little time was left. Very soon they'd take Tomoe back to the temple. But she didn't want to think about that right now.

"You probably should." But she didn't move to out of the way. She wanted this moment to last forever.

Tomoe banged on the door again.

"She's going to break down that door." He smirked at Akane.

She laughed. "I'll see you later?" Akane asked. Which was silly, of course they'd see one another. They had to take Tomoe back to the temple together.

"Definitely." He kissed again, an unhurried lingering kiss.

The banging turned into a crash, and it sounded like Tomoe was slamming her shoulder into the door. Akane had to let her in before she hurt herself.

They shared a look, and then Shin slid the door open. Tomoe almost fell flat on her face as he opened it. She caught herself at the last minute and straightened up to give Shin a look as he strolled out of the room. Tomoe turned around once he was gone and sighed, with a dreamy girlish expression. It was surprising to see Tomoe this way, she'd never expressed any interest in romance before.

"What was so urgent you burst in here first thing in the morning?" Akane said casually, as if she hadn't just been caught in bed with Shin.

"Oh no, you're not going to just ignore this. You have to explain, how'd this happen?"

"I'm not going to tell you that," Akane sputtered.

"I know what happened, I found you both naked in bed together," Tomoe said, rolling her eyes. "How did you meet? When did you get to know each other so well?" She waggled her eyebrows suggestively.

It felt like a million years since Tomoe was kidnapped. Shin had been pretending to be Shinon then. Akane blushed and busied herself dressing. She didn't want to explain to Tomoe, who was little more than a child, her carnal relationship with Shin. But she supposed it wouldn't hurt to tell her the rest of the story, minus what had happened last night.

When Akane was done telling Tomoe everything that had happened up until now, she was staring wistfully out the window. There was a small ledge, which she was perched upon. It reminded Akane of home, and how Tomoe would stare with longing out it. According to the head priestess, Tomoe was the most powerful priestess to be born in centuries. It was hard to believe her impulsive dreamer could be. And soon she'd need to return to the temple to resume her role as kamigakari.

"Then does this mean you'll be staying here with him at the dragon's palace?"

"Of course not," Akane said with a frown. She had a duty to the temple.

"But he's the dragon's general. Where else will you both go?"

Akane shook her head. "There's no us. We just had some fun..."

"Maybe not yet. But once we get settled in here, maybe you'll change your mind," Tomoe said, jumping down from the windowsill.

"We're not settling in here."

Tomoe spun to face her and her brows shot to her hairline. "Did you have another plan? I kind of like it here. I was talking to the priestess, Suzume, turns out she's the emperor's second wife's daughter, so we're sisters! She said I could stay here; the dragon will protect me. And then there's Yuuto, he's going to teach me to fight…"

"Tomoe, we're going back to the temple."

"What? But you and Shin?" she stuttered.

"What's between us doesn't change anything. You are meant to be the kamigakari."

"The head priestess was going to send me back to the palace because I had no power. You don't need to bring me back."

Akane shook her head. "The head priestess hid your power to protect you. If the yokai found out they would have killed you."

"You're a yokai."

"I am a temple guardian. And the fate of the kingdom and the war depends on you taking your place as kamigakari." She reached for Tomoe to try and comfort her, or at the very least help her see reason.

But Tomoe backed away from her, hands balled into fists at her side. "The whole reason for this stupid human and yokai war is because the kami have been gone from this world for five hundred years!"

"That's not possible." Akane waved away the very notion. "Then who has been taking the bodies of those girls, all the kamigakari before you?" Akane asked.

Tomoe's hand fell to her side as she frowned.

"See," Akane said, and slung her arm around Tomoe's shoulder. "It's going to be alright, accepting the kami is a blessing."

Tomoe rolled her shoulders and freed herself of Akane's embrace. "No. I refuse." She stormed out of the room.

"Tomoe!" Akane shouted after her retreating back.

Twenty-Two

Leaving Akane that morning had to be the hardest thing he'd ever done. The memory of her hands clawing his back left him aching for more. The halls of the dragon's palace were lit with early morning rays, and the yokai he passed in the halls bowed to him with a smile as he passed. Once they returned Tomoe to the temple, he would make a home here for Akane and himself. It might take time for her to adjust to living amongst her own kind, but he felt confident she could adapt. For so long he'd thought his suffering would never end. And now after five hundred years as Akio's dog, he was nearly free. His chest swelled with joy, so much he thought he might burst.

A kappa rushed toward him. It stooped into a low bow, nearly spilling the water in the bowl-shaped indent on top of its head.

"The dragon requests your presence," said the kappa messenger.

"He does?" Shin arched a brow. The dragon had never been formal with him. They were friends. If he had something to say, he could come to Shin himself.

He was in a good mood and he decided to play along. Shin followed the waggling, turtle shell back of the kappa. The kappa had to weave his way through the crowded palace halls. Being smaller than most yokai, this was easy for him, despite the dense crowds that swelled in the halls. Shin smiled as he squeezed past them, but got only somber expressions in return. Some didn't even bother to acknowledge him. They were too busy whispering, heads pressed close together.

The kappa led him, not to the map room, but a formal entertaining space. The scent of fresh paint and new tatami flooring tickled his nostrils as he entered. The dragon sat on a plush cushion behind a low table, a steaming tea kettle and two cups were set out. The dragon wore a blue kimono with a pattern of two dragons battling embroidered into it. His sash was a dark blue almost black and his hair had been slicked back into a tight top knot.

"What's all this about?" Shin asked.

The dragon gestured with one hand to the fat, ruby red cushion opposite him. "Take a seat."

"You're acting strange." The cushion didn't look danger-ous, but the dragon wasn't acting like himself. He'd seen this version of his old friend only when speaking with important allies, ones he was hoping to woo to his cause.

"I'm setting the mood." The dragon flashed a grin, his eyes dancing with humor. His expression smoothed. "Kenshin."

The hairs on the back of his neck stood on end. The dragon must mean business if he was using Shin's true name. A yokai's real name was secret, never spoken aloud, because it held power over them. It could be used to bind or command. In Shin's case, only two people knew his true name. The dragon and his creator, The Lady of the Forest.

He had revealed his secret name to the dragon as a sign of trust and to swear himself into the dragon's service, during the war of heaven and earth, eons ago. The dragon had never once used it.

"I would implore you, resume your place as my right hand, as my confidant and my general."

A laugh burst from his lips. "You would think you're asking me to marry you." Shin doubled over as mirth rippled through him.

The dragon watched him, his expression giving nothing away. The dragon wasn't joking around.

Shin stood straight, his eyes trying to meet his old friend's. He'd seen this look in the dragon's eyes before, only once before, when his back was against the wall.

"You're serious, aren't you?" Shin sunk down onto the cushion across from the dragon.

"I'm in desperate need of your help," the dragon said. His hands resting on the table were balled into fists. "There is a battle ahead of me that I cannot win without you."

Shin ran a thumb along the collar around his neck. For now the head priestess' binding held, and prevented him from doing Akio's bidding. "You'd want me, even after I betrayed you?"

The dragon threw his head back and laughed. "We all do selfish things for love." A shadow passed over his face, then he shook his head.

"You knew how I felt about Rin?" Shin rubbed the back of his neck.

"I have eyes, don't I?"

Shin forced a laugh. Perhaps his old feelings for Rin hadn't been as subtle as he thought.

"I wanted to talk to you about this last night. But you snuck away." He raised his eyebrows.

"What is it you want to talk about?" Shin said, trying to steer the conversation away from him and Akane.

The dragon smiled, exposing his white teeth. "I know you'd made a deal to protect Rin. And if I'm being honest, I was hurt you'd turn your back on me like that. But I think you've suffered enough. You say the word and I will skewer that pig myself to set you free."

Shin laughed, for real this time. "I never knew you cared so much."

"I need you back." His gaze was piercing. In all their years of friendship, Shin had never seen him look quite so desperate.

"I've got it figured out. I am taking the girl back to the temple, and once I return I promise to return to my old place at your side."

He'd never expected his friend to save him. The only way the dragon could free him was if he could kill Akio. But it wasn't as simple as he made it sound. Akio never left his palace. It was incredibly fortified, and he surrounded himself with the most powerful yokai. And until Shin broke free, he could command Shin to attack his friend. The huntsman had almost broken through the head priestess' bindings as it was.

The dragon smiled. "I'm glad to hear it. But don't be gone too long, or I'll come looking for you."

The dragon poured Shin a cup of tea, which Shin took, taking a slow sip. It had a pleasant floral aroma.

"Now are you going to tell me what's going on with you and that she-wolf?"

Shin choked on his tea. He coughed as he set his cup down.

Across the table, the dragon smirked as he slapped the table. "I knew there was something between you."

Shin took another sip of his tea to avoid answering. The dragon watched him all the while. Shin knew that glint in his eye. He wanted details.

"I don't know what you're talking about," Shin said, after draining his cup. He reached for the kettle to refill, if only to have something to do with his hands.

"It was her that had you so distracted last night, wasn't it?"

"She's uncomfortable in a crowd. I wanted to make sure she was alright, that's all," Shin replied with a shrug. It was all so fresh, he wanted to keep it to himself, just for a little while longer.

"Do you really think I'm going to fall for that?" The dragon gave him a look. Back in the day they'd often bragged of their sexual exploits to one another. But perhaps holding back information was the wrong tactic because now the dragon was like a dog on the scent.

"It's not what you think."

"Did you take her to your bed last night?" the dragon asked with a salacious grin as he leaned across the table.

Shin bristled, they may be friends but even he had his limits. "Are you trying to pick a fight?"

The dragon whistled long and low. "You've got it bad, my friend."

There was nothing he could say that wouldn't get him in too deep. Shin shook his head and stood. "I'm sure you've got other matters to attend to."

"Don't be like that," the dragon called as Shin headed to the door.

Before he could escape, the dragon caught up and slung his arm around Shin's shoulder.

"I mean no offense. I'm just happy for you. I gave up on Rin for you, after all."

"You gave up on Rin because you were bored."

The dragon shrugged. "We both were. But enough about my old flames. What about you? How is she between the blankets?"

Shin slid the door open and stepped out of his grasp. He turned with his back to the open door.

"I would appreciate you not speak that way about the woman I love."

The dragon's eyes widened. Shin hadn't thought it such a strange proclamation. Then again it was the first time he was saying it out loud. But it felt right, being with Akane felt right.

"Can we talk?" Akane said from behind him.

"I'll leave you lovebirds alone." The dragon slid past them and out the door. As he strolled down the hall he whistled to himself.

There was a crimson stain across Akane's cheeks. She must have heard him. It wasn't the ideal way to confess his feelings to her, but he supposed it was going to be said one way or another.

"We can do more than talk." He waggled his eyebrows and took her hand, drawing her into the formal meeting room. He'd never done it in here, but there was a first for everything.

She looked at her feet. "I had a lot of fun last night."

He pulled her close, pressing her chest flush against him. "There's even more fun to be had."

There was so much more he wanted to say. But he couldn't find the right words. That she drove him mad with desire, that he'd never found a woman who balanced him so completely, who challenged him as a man and as a wolf. She pulled back in his embrace, putting a hands breath distance between them.

"I appreciate your feelings, but—"

A cold chill swept over him. No, not again.

He dropped his hold on her taking a step back.

"But you don't love me, is that it?"

Her brown eyes fixed upon him, darting across his face. Then she looked away, gaze once more on her feet. "I have a duty to the temple."

There was a sinking feeling in the pit of his stomach. Had he been a fool to even hope for a future with her?

"I see."

"I'm sorry." She reached for him, but he stepped outside her grasp.

"No. I understand."

They stood in silence. Shin studied the table where the tea kettle and cups remained. The water had cooled and the cups were empty. His cup had a small hair fracture. Inside he felt similar cracks spreading over his heart. Perhaps this was his lot in life, to forever long for love and never have that desire fulfilled. He wouldn't beg her to love him, he had more dignity than that.

"Then I suppose it's time we brought you back to your temple." He turned toward the door.

"Shin."

He stopped in his tracks. Hopeful. Desperate. She would take back what she'd said.

"Thank you, for everything."

Inside he was shattered.

"Don't thank me, I only did it to get my freedom." He walked out of the room before she'd see just how completely she'd destroyed him.

THEY SET OUT FOR THE TEMPLE. AKANE AND SHIN HADN'T spoken a word since they left. She stayed close to Tomoe, who walked with her head hung low. Any joy he might have felt at his impending freedom was muted by his heartbreak. Each step felt like weights were attached to his feet. Even looking at Akane felt like the point of a knife to his gut. So instead, he scouted the forest up ahead in wolf form. Letting his grief roll off him as the forest floor passed beneath his paws.

The forest was eerily quiet. Leaves crunched under his paws, echoing back at him. Then like a whisper, he felt an immense power brush against him. Shin spun around, racing back toward Akane and Tomoe.

When he found them again, Akane had shifted into her wolf form and she stood her ground in front of Tomoe. At least fifty yokai surrounded them on all sides. Shin rushed in, knocking them down with powerful paws. But they only tightened ranks, their sheer numbers holding him back.

Inside the circle Akane was snapping at anyone who came near, while Tomoe picked up anything she could get her hands on to toss at the assailants. The bitter scent of metal hit him like a blow to the face. Shin rolled, a second before the ax was embedded into the ground where he'd just stood.

Teeth bared, Shin faced the huntsman.

Akane roared and charged the yokai. They swarmed over her, climbing onto her back, weighing her down with their sheer numbers. Tomoe had picked up a stick and had started beating on the nearby yokai to no avail. A lizard yokai snuck up behind her and pinned her arms behind her head.

Shin pushed through the crowd, but they made an impassable wall of flesh.

A lizard yokai had climbed onto Akane's back and his jaws were hovering over her throat. The poison would kill her in an instant. She squirmed against the boar and monkey yokai who had pinned her to the ground, but she couldn't shake them off.

"Don't hurt her," Shin growled. "It's me Akio wants."

The huntsman yanked his ax from the ground and returned it to his holder on his back.

"Fight me and they both die," the huntsman said. His voice lacked any inflection. He stepped toward Shin, and each footstep seemed to slam into his chest. The collar felt as if it had shrunk and was choking him. It was better for him to die than Akane get hurt.

The huntsman stood before Shin, his dark gaze a bottomless pit. He crouched as he grasped hold of Shin's collar.

"You never were going to escape."

He closed a fist over the collar. Fire spread across it, and flames licked against his neck. Shin did not turn away. He faced it.

"Shin, no!" Akane cried out his name. She rocked against her captors to no avail.

The bindings the witch had put upon it were turned to ash. Shin collapsed to the ground as Akio's power over him pulsed through him.

"You will lure the dragon to Akio, and there you will kill him."

"You don't have to do this, Shin," Akane shouted.

"If you fail, they will die. If you warn the dragon, they will die. If you disobey in any way, they will die."

Shin lowered his head to the ground. "Understood. I will do as I am commanded."

TWENTY-THREE

Blindfolded and hands bound behind their backs, Tomoe and Akane were transported in what she assumed was a palanquin. She was laying on a hard surface, her back to Tomoe. They jostled and rolled as they traversed over different terrain. The only indication of where they were was the changing scent. The salt of the sea faded quickly and was replaced by musky pines. They moved quickly, impossibly so, over great distances. Tomoe had found Akane's hand and squeezed it in a death grip. The palanquin came to a jolting stop and Akane and Tomoe slid forward, nearly slamming into the wall of the palanquin. Tomoe whimpered softly as she lost hold of Akane's hand.

"Don't worry. I'm here." Akane soothed her the best she could. All the while her mind was racing. If she could get these bindings free, she might be able to surprise their captors and overpower them. But having Tomoe was a liability. Her first responsibility was to protect Tomoe. Could she fight and protect her at the same time? She wasn't certain and she didn't want to take a risk. The best option was to wait for the opportune moment.

Wherever they were, it smelled familiar and the energy of the place prickled against her skin. The doors of the palanquin swung open and the stench of yokai filled her nostrils. They grabbed Tomoe first and she screamed.

"Tomoe!" Akane shouted.

"Shut her up," one of the yokai growled.

Akane flopped toward the sound of Tomoe's voice. Her head swiveled around, searching for her with scent and sound. She called out, "Tomoe, don't worry. I'm here."

Something hit Akane hard against the back of her head.

"Quiet, you," said a disembodied voice.

She slumped forward and fell into the arms of her captor. Then she was dragged out of the palanquin. The warmth of the sun prickled along her skin and there was a faint hint of jasmine on the air. Nearby, Tomoe sniffled. Judging by the echoing footsteps, they were being led down some sort of corridor. Akane tilted her head to and fro, catching their scent. There were fewer people holding onto them.

But if she were inside a palace, getting them both out would be a challenge. If only she could see where they were going.

They came to an abrupt halt, forced to their knees, and then their blindfolds were removed. Akane blinked into the bright light surrounding her. The room was enormous. The ceiling reached up to the heavens and pillars lined both sides. At the far end, an enormous boar consumed the space. Around him yokai attendants held platters of food and large saucers of sake aloft. He snatched up the saucer and drank deeply from it, dribbling onto his chin. He smacked his lips and dropped the saucer down, almost sending the cup-bearer tipping over.

He smiled at Akane, revealing yellowing teeth. "You are the one then, the trespasser?"

This must be Akio, the monster who Shin said was his master. She had a feeling that her trespassing wasn't the real problem, but Shin's disobedience. If Tomoe weren't here, she'd transform and rip his throat out. But the room was crawling with yokai. She'd never get out alive.

"It was me who came onto your land. Punish me how you will, but the girl has nothing to do with this. Let her go." Akane gestured toward Tomoe who'd squatted and folded over, clutching her knees to her chest.

"Doesn't she? Why would Shin go to such lengths for this girl then?" The boar leaned forward, his beady black eyes gleaming.

Akane felt a cold ripple down her spine. "He did it for me. If you want to get back at Shin, I'm the one you want."

The boar threw his head back and laughed. "You can't be that much of a fool, can you?"

Akane only glared in response. She refused to fall for his taunting. He would try and trick her into revealing Tomoe's power.

"He may try and escape, but he belongs to me. And like a good dog, he delivered you both to me." He nodded toward Tomoe who was trembling uncontrollably. Akane wished she could reach out and comfort her. Instead she squeezed her hand into a fist at her side.

"Shin would never do that," she said with assurance.

The boar and everyone around the room started to laugh, until they were surrounded by the eerie echo of their voice.

"You've fallen for his charms, haven't you? There isn't a woman here who hasn't been to his bed."

The female attendants all nodded their heads in agreement. Akane's chest clenched. It wasn't true. He said he loved her. She was the one who pushed him away. It wasn't that she didn't love him, she did. But she wouldn't put love over duty.

"You're lying," she said.

The boar's smile was much too pleased. It made her skin crawl.

"Take them to the cells until I decide what to do with them," Akio said with a wave of his hoof.

They grabbed her by the shoulders and she didn't even fight them as they led her out. She kept her eyes open, studying the layout, trying to form an escape plan. She had to get out of here before Shin came back with the dragon. They went down a spiral staircase that led into the ground. The air stank of mildew and moisture. At the end of a long hallway was a single door where they were tossed inside. Tomoe curled up into a ball and rocked back and forth.

"Are they going to turn me into one of those monsters?" she asked Akane. Her voice was thin and reedy.

She wrapped her arm around Tomoe's shoulder.

"I'll think of something, I'll find a way to get us out of here, don't worry." But how could she? There seemed no easy way out.

Tomoe cried until she fell into an exhausted sleep, her head pillowed on Akane's lap. She tangled her hands in the girl's hair, planning their escape. *I will get you out of here, I promise.* They couldn't leave them in here forever. They'd have to come for them eventually, and when they did, she'd transform into a wolf and tear out their throats. Just another reason to be thankful for Shin. And what had she done to thank him for his kindness and love? She turned her back on him. If she hadn't, would they be here right now? She couldn't think about that. Better to focus on her escape.

Hours passed, maybe a night. It was hard to tell in the complete darkness of the cell. The darkness started to fade, and a light approached. Akane gently set Tomoe on the ground next to her. She woke up anyway and looked at Akane with a sleepy gaze. Akane pressed her finger to her lips and crouched down low, preparing to transform. But the transition did not come easily. Perhaps she was just out of practice. The light was right outside their door. She decided to use her bare hands if it came down to it.

The door opened and she sprung for her captors. As she did, an invisible force tossed her back away from them. She skidded along the ground before leaping up and attempting it again, only to collide once more with an invisible barrier.

"Don't waste your time, your powers are useless in here," a boar yokai at the head of the group said.

At the back of the group, a yokai's hands glowed as he created a barrier around them.

The yokai marched into the room with practiced indifference. Akane pushed Tomoe behind her as they backed away from them. Snarling and snapping like a feral beast, she tried to keep them back. But they were not easily intimidated. They grabbed her arms and feet, pinning her to the ground while she arched her back and growled.

"Akane!" Tomoe cried and rushed toward her, but two more yokai grabbed her and held her back.

Whatever magic had made the barrier was also keeping Akane from accessing her spiritual energy. They clamped shackles on Akane's wrists and around her throat, much like the collar Shin wore but made of dark, black material. It was like nothing she'd felt before and it cut off the flow of energy inside her, leaving her weak and docile. She sagged in her bonds, defeated. The leader grabbed the chain that hooked onto the front of her collar and tugged, pulling her after him. Tomoe tried to follow once her captors let her go, but they slammed the door in her face, leaving her in darkness alone.

"Akane!" She screeched again.

Akane tried to twist around but they yanked her forward.

"Don't leave me," Tomoe cried as Akane disappeared up the stairs.

"I'll get us out, don't worry. I'll be back," Akane shouted.

Then her captor yanked on the chain, nearly choking her. "Quiet."

Back up the stairs and through a series of twisting corridors, Akane tried to memorize her path, but when she looked over her shoulder the pathway changed and was something else entirely.

"Don't even waste time thinking about escape," the guard said. "The palace changes all the time."

Akane growled at him, snapping her teeth and the man backed away while his companion laughed.

"This one has spirit."

"Akio will break her of that soon enough," said the first.

They dragged her back into the audience room. The boar was where she'd last seen him, but he wasn't alone. He had a visitor. Standing at the front of the room, her back upright, not bent as she had last seen her, was the head priestess.

"Head Priestess!" Akane cried and tugged on her chain, as she attempted to get closer to her.

The head priestess looked Akane up and down, before turning back to the boar.

"Where is the girl? Don't play your tricks on me, Akio."

"But isn't this your little spy you sent to check up on me?"

The head priestess sniffed. "Don't change the subject, you have the girl, I want her back."

"What does a human girl matter to you?"

The head priestess' lips curled up.

"Head Priestess, I'm sorry. I tried to protect her—" Akane attempted to interject.

"Quiet, you fool." The head priestess' voice cracked across her like a smack to the face, she'd never spoken that way to her before. There was something different about her, it was like she was a stranger. The head priestess turned her back on Akane to look at Akio again. "What do you want for the girl?" the head priestess asked.

"What about your little spy?" Akio nodded toward Akane.

"She is no concern of mine, any longer. Do with her as you wish."

"Head Priestess?" Akane asked. Surely she was here to save them. She knew this woman. She still remembered the day she came to the shrine. She wouldn't just leave her here. This had to be a trick, to deceive the guardian.

The head priestess turned and marched toward Akane. She stood before her and narrowed her eyes. "You've been nothing but trouble. First you influenced Mei, and now

Tomoe. I sent you here hoping the guardian would catch you, but you returned, like the dog you are with your tail between your legs. You are worthless to me; do you understand now?"

Akane blinked, the words settling like a stone on her chest.

The head priestess turned back around to Akio. Akane watched without really seeing. Their words washed over her like the waves on the shore.

"What will it take to get the girl back?" the head priestess repeated.

"First, tell me what you want her for." Akio replied, his beady eyes narrowed.

The head priestess sighed. "You know why I want her."

"I want to hear you say it." He looked toward Akane with a salacious grin. Was this his way of torturing Akane? To twist the knife? He had known who Tomoe was from the start. Akane was never able to protect her.

"She's my next vessel. Satisfied? Now let's make a deal."

"What vessel? Tomoe is meant to be the kamigakari, isn't she?" Akane asked.

They both ignored her as if she hadn't spoken at all.

"I'm surprised you've gone this long. Your current body is falling apart around you," Akio said, leaning forward to inspect the head priestess.

"There were circumstances that kept me from shedding this pathetic shell," she replied curtly. "Now where is the girl?"

"There are many who'd want a girl with her power for themselves." Akio scratched his chin with his hoof.

"But if you waste it on the darkness' stupid games, you will lose a chance at an alliance with the humans."

"I'm listening," Akio said, leaning forward, eagerly lapping at her words.

"That girl is not merely a priestess, but a princess, and the intended to the future emperor. When I take her body, I will have the ear of the emperor. And a crucial ally in defeating the dragon for you at last."

Akio pressed his hooves together. "It is a tempting offer."

He looked at Akane. Her head was spinning. The head priestess' words were not her own, surely. But then she saw the subtle shift in her aura. It was familiar. It was the kami's aura, or the aura she had always assumed belonged to the kami. Why had she never seen it before? The head priestess, or whoever she was, had been impersonating the kami this entire time.

"It's a deal." He snapped his fingers and, in an instant, Tomoe sat on the ground before them. She blinked into the light. First, she saw the head priestess, and then Akane shackled to the ground.

"Head Priestess, you came for us," she cried out and motioned to grab Akane, but as she did, the head priestess grabbed her by the wrist, holding her back.

"You're coming with me, girl."

"But what about Akane?"

"She is no longer our concern." She turned and pulled her out of the room. Tomoe tried to pull away but couldn't quite free herself of the head priestess' grip. She reached for Akane. A tear rolled down Akane's cheek as Akio stood and walked toward her, in his hand a metal collar.

"You're mine now, dog."

Twenty-Four

Every heartbeat, each step it took to get to Akio's palace was as excruciating as it was long. After telling the dragon that Tomoe was the key to freeing himself of Akio's spell, the dragon had not hesitated to help him save Akane and Tomoe. Though he desperately wished he had declined as he had before. Worse yet, Rin and Hikaru had insisted on joining along, as well as the fire-wielding priestess, Suzume. Would Akio have him kill them all? He wasn't ready to give into Akio just yet. He hadn't broken any of his commands, per se. Getting through the forest's defenses had been easy. Akio had made it so, but Shin had to pretend he knew every trail and hidden passageway better than anyone else. Now they stood before the final obstacle. The palace was cut off from the forest with a miles-deep canyon. The only way across was a single rope bridge.

"Never thought I'd be back here again," Hikaru said.

Shin looked at him, remembering that day hundreds of years ago when they'd come together to save Rin. It was also the day he'd given himself over to Akio for Rin's sake.

Shin placed his hand on Hikaru's shoulder. They'd never gotten a chance to get to know one another. And Shin had spent centuries resenting the man for loving Rin. They suited one another, he could see that now. And if they failed and Shin was forced to kill the dragon, he'd likely never get the chance to know them better.

"I'm glad it's you here beside me," Shin said with a forced smile. He'd wracked his brain to find a way around Akio's command, but he'd planned for every incidental. As long as he had Akane, Shin had to go through with it.

Hikaru gave him a faint smile in return. The dragon pushed between them and slung an arm around Shin's shoulder. "Aren't you forgetting someone?"

It was just like his old friend to get jealous. And it only made what he had to do that much harder. He had to get to Akio first, to try and kill him before he could force his command upon him. But the dragon trusted him implicitly. The collar around his neck burned, as if Akio's invisible hand was clenched around his throat.

"Are you ready?" Shin asked the dragon.

The dragon replied with a fierce smile. Ice crystals spread out from his feet, and there was a definite chill in the air. The dragon's affinity was water, and when he lost his temper or unfurled his full power, it had a tendency to freeze everything around him. "I've been waiting for a chance to face Akio for centuries," he said.

The dragon and Akio's grudge went back longer than either of them could remember. Sometimes Shin wondered if they even remembered what had started it. Rin had assumed her kitsune form, her flaming feet scorching the earth beneath her and turning the dragon's ice into puddles.

"Let's go." Shin growled as he shifted into his true wolf form.

As a massive white wolf, he led the charge. He only needed the dragon to follow. He had a plan to get rid of the rest of them. They rushed the bridge, but as they got closer three flame yokai emerged from a sudden puff of smoke and blocked their path. The dragon transformed into his true serpentine form, flying into the air up above and sending a blast of ice to freeze the guards into giant blocks of ice. Shin, Rin, Hikaru, and Suzume at the rear stormed the bridge. As soon as they stepped foot on it, the bridge swung perilously. A strong wind had picked up, triggered by their invasion. It was one of many enchantments that guarded the palace against outsiders. Shin had prepared for this. They just had to get across quickly.

Then from the back, Suzume shouted. "They're breaking free."

The flame yokai had broken out of their icy prisons and were burning the ropes of the bridge. Suzume ran toward them in an attempt to stop them, but it was too late. One of the ropes snapped and the bridge tipped sideways. With seconds to spare, Shin transformed into his human form so he could grab onto the remaining rope. Suzume was not so lucky, she tumbled over the side down into the canyon below.

"Suzume!" the dragon roared and dove down after her.

They all held their breath, watching as Suzume faded into the darkness below. The dragon was a blur of blue streaking after her.

"He won't let her fall," Hikaru said, confidently. "We have problems of our own."

The fire yokai had regrouped and were shooting fiery blasts in their direction. One of them had caught fire to the remaining rope. Their only choice was to shimmy along the remaining rope and hope the fire would go out. About halfway across the bridge, the second rope snapped, sending the bridge swinging toward the canyon wall. The dangling ends of the rope hung over the bottomless pit.

Hikaru, at the top, started to climb but his progress was encumbered by the flame yokai's attacks, which were carried across by the wind. They all would have plummeted to their death, but the dragon rose up from the depths of the canyon with the priestess Suzume riding on his back.

"Get into the palace. I'll follow," the dragon growled as he shot ice at the flame yokai.

They scampered up the side, using the bridge like a ladder, Hikaru giving Rin and Shin a hand up. Once they were at the top, Shin hesitated. He hadn't accounted for the dragon's attachment to the priestess. But at least it kept the dragon behind, giving him more time to reach Akio alone.

"This way," Shin said before gesturing for them to follow. He knew these twisted hallways like the back of his hand but if they got lost within them, perhaps he could spare them. He took them down tangled corridors, up stairwells that brought them to underground chambers, and through doorways which opened onto gardens. They passed through a garden dominated by a huge jasmine bush whose trunk was as thick as a tree's. It was there that the huntsman found them.

"Don't waste your time, Shin," the huntsman said as if he didn't particularly care one way or another.

Rin lurched forward, teeth bared, while Hikaru rapid fired arrows at the huntsman and the yokai surrounding him. The huntsman drew his ax, swinging it in a wide arc around him. Rin skidded backward, inches from being sliced in half.

"I'm afraid I cannot let any of you pass," the huntsman said in a bored tone.

Rin growled in response, like a wild beast. But that was just a distraction. While he was busy watching her, Hikaru had gotten into position and fired at the huntsman. He spun just in time, using his ax to deflect the shot. It ricocheted off it and impaled into a nearby pillar.

"This is futile," the huntsman said.

Rin rushed him on his right, while Hikaru fired on the left. The huntsman leaped out of the way of Rin and Hikaru's attacks with ease.

"I have no desire to kill you, but I will," the huntsman drawled.

What he hadn't been counting on, was Shin sneaking up behind him.

"Well, I have no problem killing you."

He spun, swinging his ax at Shin with less grace than usual. Shin dodged, coming up and knocking him off his feet. The huntsman stumbled backward and that's when

Rin came back again. The huntsman was being driven backward, away from the doorway he'd been guarding.

"Go, we've got it from here," Hikaru said, as he gave Rin cover fire. She continued to draw the huntsman away and kept him distracted long enough for Shin to slip away.

He resisted the urge to look back and make sure Rin was safe. He had to trust that she could take care of herself, and she had Hikaru with her anyway. Beyond the doorway was another long hall. There were no tricks here, just a pair of double doors, which led into Akio's audience hall. Akio's stink permeated everything and mixed in was the faintness thread of Akane's scent, spiked with fear.

Shin burst through the double doors, teeth bared and prepared to tear Akio's throat out himself. If he killed him first, he could save Akane. Akio was seated in his usual place, sipping sake with casual indifference, as if his palace wasn't under attack at this very moment. He did not turn to Shin as he made his dramatic entrance. Wrapped around his hoof was a chain, and at the end, a white wolf, her head drooping and defeated.

Akane.

Shin ran toward Akio, snarling, but before he could get more than a few feet, fire burned him from the inside. It brought him to the ground and he convulsed in pain. Akane, on the chain, looked up and whimpered. Akio yanked the chain, and it pulled her off her feet and left her sprawling on the ground where she lay motionless as if dead.

Akio stood up and approached Shin. Pain throbbed through Shin at every step. This was only a taste of what Akio would do to him. He'd endured much worse. Akio's favorite past time was psychological torture. Akio loomed over Shin, a smile on his face.

"You thought you could escape me?" He laughed, throwing his head back. "I should have known when you let her go you would betray me."

"It's not betrayal if I was never loyal to you," Shin croaked.

The pain increased by tenfold, blinding him, dulling all his senses. Stars danced in front of his eyes. He was nothing but pain, all of it radiating outward from his collar.

"You're losing your touch, Akio, that tickled," Shin taunted, his voice husky from the pain he couldn't quite mask.

He was rewarded with another shot of pain pinging through his entire body.

"Learn when you're beat and stay down, dog. You failed." Akio gloated.

Shin hadn't come this far just to bow down and just let him torture him. He licked his lips and tasted blood. He must have bit his tongue. With effort, Shin stood up and lifted his chin in defiance to Akio, challenging him to do it again. Whatever torture he wanted to put him through, he'd endure it all to save her. He just had to wait for the dragon. He'd end this.

"Is that how you want to play it?" Akio turned over to Akane. Her body convulsed as the same pain he'd inflicted on Shin tore her apart.

Shin saw nothing at all, he was nothing but a beast of reaction. He launched himself toward Akio again, but before he could attack, he was knocked back onto the ground by Akio's blow, and then pinned to the ground, frozen in place, forced to watch Akane's cry of agony. It tore into his heart, shredding him into a thousand pieces.

"Stop," Shin groaned.

Akio's laughter bounced off the ceiling, cruel and mocking.

"Stop," Shin said louder as he crawled closer to Akane. "Whatever you want, I'll give it to you. Just leave her alone."

Akio turned to him for the first time. "You love her, do you? You're more a fool than I thought. I'm not done punishing you. Not until your job is complete. Come with me."

Akio yanked on the chain around Akane's collar and dragged her out of the room. He had no choice but to follow. They left the audience chamber and went down a hallway. For everyone else, the palace changed. But Akio's power was tied into the palace itself and he bent it to his whim. They entered a strange room, the likes of which Shin had never seen before. There was no ceiling, but high walls and columns surrounded it on all sides.

Akio tilted his head upward, toward the sky. "Ah, here he comes now."

The ground beneath Shin's feet shook. A roar ripped through the sky as the dragon arrived, dark clouds heavy with rain cloaking his body as he twisted in the sky.

Shin stared upward toward his friend and then toward Akane, who was watching him with wide, fear-filled eyes. This had been Akio's plan all along. It was likely why he let Shin escape for as long as he did. The dragon and Akio's feud ended today, one way or another. Shin couldn't disobey Akio's command. He would have to fight the dragon. But he wasn't going to kill his friend either. The only way out of this was death.

The dragon drew closer but hovered in the air, just above where the roof should have been.

"You came to retrieve your dog?" Akio taunted him.

"I came to get repayment for all your gifts, Akio," the dragon replied. The priestess wasn't with him. He must have left her behind. It was probably for the best. Shin didn't want her to become another casualty. He hoped the dragon and her were happy together. It was too bad he wouldn't be able to retake his place as dragon's general.

Akio laughed. "You think you can defeat me, weak as you are?"

"It won't take much to destroy you." The dragon dove toward Akio, who smiled as he approached.

With a wave of his hoof, the ceiling came down, trapping the dragon inside. They were plunged into darkness. It took only a few moments for his eyes to adjust to the dark. Then compelled by Akio's command, Shin lunged in front of Akio to block the dragon's attack. The dragon reared back and flew toward the ceiling.

"Shin, what are you doing?"

"I'm sorry," Shin said as he growled and clawed at the dragon.

The dragon ran from him, keeping to the ceiling just out of reach.

"What has gotten into you?" The dragon growled as he darted out of Shin's reach.

Akio's laughter echoed all around them, followed by rumbling as the ceiling was lowered, forcing the dragon downward and closer to them. Unable to retreat any longer, the dragon transformed back into his humanoid form. He landed on the ground in front of Shin, a blade of ice in his hand.

"I don't want to fight you," he said to Shin.

If he had the power, he would have apologized to his friend. But Akio's command burned through him, unable to be disobeyed. He launched into the air and lunged for the dragon. He blocked his attack, sending Shin backward.

Over and over they clashed together. The dragon defending, and Shin attacking, not holding back.

"Kill me. It's the only way to stop this," Shin growled.

The dragon looked at him with sorrow in his eyes. They both knew it was true. When the dragon came for him this time, he didn't hold back. He thrust forward, and the ice pierced Shin in the chest. He collapsed to the ground.

Twenty-Five

Shin fell in slow motion and time froze for Akane as her heart shattered into a thousand pieces. The wolf inside her roared. She lurched forward, pulling the chain taut. Akio attempted to yank her back, but the force of her rage snapped it and she rushed toward the dragon. He stood over Shin's body, his blood still dripping from the dragon's blade. Akane slammed into him, knocking him off his feet and pressed her paws to his chest as he stared up at her wide-eyed.

"You killed him," she snarled.

"He did it to save you," he snapped back, grief making his voice thick.

Her jaws circled the dragon's neck. It wasn't a good enough excuse, nothing he said could have soothed the beast within. "Give me one reason not to kill you," she growled.

"I'm not the one you want revenge from, it's him." He nodded behind him toward Akio. "He's the one who pitted us against one another."

The rational part of her knew that was the truth. But the wolf in her believed only what her eyes saw. Akane hesitated, torn between two thoughts. And rising up from the murky depths of her conflicted psyche was one thought, *Shin wouldn't want this.*

Akio laughed and clapped his hands together. "I may have lost one mutt, but I've gained a loyal one at least it seems."

"Help me get revenge," the dragon said, his eyes beseeching.

It was then her decision was made. Akane spun to face Akio, and sprung toward him, fueled by her pent up grief and rage. She channeled it all into raw power. Blindsided by her speed, Akio only had enough time to lift his arm up in a lame defensive move. She latched onto him, pulling him backward and onto the ground. The ground rumbled as he came crashing down. Akio's eyes were wide with shock, only for a moment, however. He held out his hoof, and raw energy coalesced. He twisted around and slammed it into Akane, and the force was like an explosion, sending her flying through the air before she crashed back down on the ground in a heap. Stunned, she lay on the ground in a daze, unable to move.

The room echoed with thunder as Akio got back to his feet. "I suppose I'll have to finish this myself," he said, facing the dragon who'd gotten back up as well.

The air vibrated with energy, and along the ceiling rain clouds formed, before bursting apart in sheets of rain which blinded Akane to everything else. Water pooled on the floor and soaked her clothes and hair. And yet she couldn't rise from her lying position. This was all her fault. First Tomoe and now Shin. Why was it those she loved were doomed to die? If only she had trusted him sooner, done something to intervene, he would still be here. She squeezed her eyes shut tight, trying to fight the tears that spilled despite her best efforts to hold them back.

Then a cold nose pressed against her cheek. Akane cracked an eye open and saw a glowing white figure looming over her. Blood stained his white coat, but the gash in his chest had started to heal and was no longer bleeding. He licked away her tears. In a rush she grabbed onto the scruff of his neck, burying her face in it. Words were tangled up in her throat. He was alive? This wasn't a dream, was it?

The room shook as lightning flashed across the room. In that brief flash, Akane saw over Shin's shoulder as Akio reached for something in his pocket. He tossed whatever it was down his throat and then his aura changed, expanding outward, filling up the space and his size doubled, so that his head pressed against the ceiling and his width blocked most her view. The dragon thrust at Akio with a sword, but he caught it by the blade and yanked it from the dragon's hand, tossing it behind him. It skidded a few feet from them, and Shin stared at the blade for a moment before his eyes slid over to Akio and the dragon.

"While you've slept for centuries, I've been gathering power. Now I will have what is rightfully mine," Akio crowed as he shot a blast of his power at the dragon, who narrowly rolled out of the way.

The guardian seemed in no rush and he chased after the dragon, lazily sending him skittering across the room. There was no escape. Shin transformed into his human visage and reached for the discarded weapon.

Akane grabbed his hand to stop him.

Shin met her gaze, holding it for a moment. There were so many things she wanted and needed to say. *Don't go, I almost lost you once.* The words were on the tip of her tongue.

Shin gently removed her hand from his before walking over to pick up the sword off the ground. Akane watched him go, her heart in her throat. Distracted by chasing the dragon, Akio did not notice Shin come up behind him until the hilt of the dragon's blade was sunk deep into his back. Akio turned, eyes wide with shock as he looked at Shin, who removed the blade with a wet pop. There seemed to be a question on Akio's lips that was never uttered. Because at the same time, the dragon transformed once more into his serpentine body. He swung his tail, knocking Akio off his feet and flat on his back, blood pooling around him. Shin approached, blade in hand.

For a heartbeat everything stood still. Shin, splattered in blood and gore, stood over Akio. His eyes were dark, feral, terrifying, but also achingly sad. He didn't enjoy killing, she knew that, but it had to be done. With one merciful swipe, he separated Akio's head from his shoulders.

The sword slid from Shin's hands and he knelt down on the ground. The dragon resumed his humanoid form and placed his hand on Shin's shoulder. She held her breath waiting for him, wondering if he would snap, lose control of his wolf in the same way she had once been disconnected from the core of herself. And then he turned toward her, and all that remained was grief. She rushed toward him and gathered him up into her arms, knowing the pain that tore him apart.

He clung to her back, holding onto her as if she would keep him from sinking.

"It's over now," she soothed, pushing his hair back away from his face.

He looked at her, eyes large as he searched her face. "Is it?"

And she knew then that it would never truly be over. The scars Akio had inflicted on his soul would always remain. But more than anyone, she knew what it meant to live with those haunting memories.

"You're free, and I'm here. That's all that matters."

"I'm sorry you had to go through this." His eyes searched hers while he clung to her as if she'd disappear any second.

She'd been a fool to push him away. He'd been willing to die for her. She kissed him in response. And they were melded together so tightly it was impossible to say where one stopped and the other started. She was home in his arms, this was where she belonged.

"I hate to ruin this touching moment, but we've got a problem," the dragon said as he pointed to the ceiling which was dropping pieces of debris down upon their heads.

A nearby column tipped over and would have crushed them, had Shin not pulled her out of the way at the last moment.

"The palace is falling apart now that the guardian is dead. We have to get out of here!" Shin shouted to the dragon who was on the other side of the fallen column.

He nodded and headed for a nearby door, but as Shin and Akane motioned to follow the same way, more chunks of ceiling fell down blocking their path.

"This way," Shin tugged on her hand, pulling her the opposite way of the dragon, back in the direction they'd come from, toward the guardian's audience hall.

When they entered the audience hall, the ground started to shake. On the far side of the room was another door and that's where they ran for. Just as they crossed the threshold, there was a loud cracking sound. Akane turned just as the floor split in half, and the dais where Akio had once sat cracked in two, pillows and saucers spilling down into it. The servants were long gone, they'd likely already fled for their own safety. On two legs they were too slow to outrun the destruction falling down around them. Shin's bushy brown hair was dusted with white plaster.

"We'll have to shift," Shin said, looking at her with brows furrowed.

She wished she could kiss him for that. But now wasn't the time.

"I'll be fine, don't worry," she said as she transformed into her wolf form. The ground gave another tremor and urged them forward. Down another hallway, they ran into three different yokai, all running in different directions. No one knew which way to go now that Akio's magic was receding.

"Follow me," Shin growled at them.

A few did, others went their own way. One yokai that ignored Shin, turned a corner and moments later they heard him scream. Akane looked over her shoulder and saw the jagged broken end of a stairway that had split and opened up into another pit.

"Don't look back," Shin warned. And Akane turned her gaze forward. There was nothing they could do for them now.

Their path led them into a garden, untouched by the destruction which was sweeping the rest of the palace. White petals scattered on the ground like fresh snow, and even more drifting down in a flurry. The air here hummed with energy.

"This place was the anchor of his power," Shin explained. "This will be the last place to fall." He turned in a slow circle, there were several pathways down which they could go. But he seemed hesitant. She'd never seen him uncertain before, and she tried to squash her fear at that thought.

She pressed close to Shin as the ground started to buck and bend again. It felt as if the entire place would flip over itself.

"This way." He nodded his head toward a nearby door.

As they passed through more tangled passageways, Shin led with confidence. But after several minutes, they returned back to the garden once again.

"Why are we here again?" one of the yokai who'd been following them asked.

Shin paced in circles. "The magic is drawing in on itself, it's bringing everything back here."

"How do we escape?" Akane asked, panic rising in her chest. She pushed it down, she had to trust.

"We try a different route," he said, with a note of uncertainty in his voice.

Shin rushed forward and chased after him, upstairs and then down again, they seemed to go on forever, but surely they'd be near the exit now. But after several minutes of searching they arrived once again at the tree.

The space had shrunk. She was certain of it. The walls were closing in.

"This is ridiculous," said one of the yokai.

"Be patient, there has to be a way out," Shin warned.

But they didn't heed his advice and rushed through the same doorway they'd just exited from. A few seconds later they heard a blood-curdling scream.

The remaining yokai shared terrified looks, but no one else tried to run away.

Akane's breathing came quick and fierce, her heart racing. What happened if the entire palace imploded?

Shin paced in circles, and then thinking out loud he said, "This tree was the original forest guardian, Akio stole its power to become what he is. Now that he's dead, the tree is regaining its power and it's bringing everything into itself."

Akane looked at the tree. When she stared it, she swore she almost heard a song floating on the wind, a melody which was drawing her in, it made her want to close her eyes, lay down and sleep...

Shin nipped at her neck. "Don't get too close to it. If you do it will pull you in and absorb your power with it."

She shook her head and looked away. That answered what happened if the tree imploded.

"Let's try this, we'll go across the rooftops," Shin said. The walls had started to crumble, making them easier to scale. In a few jumps, they were on the rooftops. In the distance she could see the edge of the palace, and the forest beyond. But, no matter how far they ran, they couldn't get any closer.

"It's no use," said one of the yokai who sat down on the ground.

"Don't sit down, we have to keep moving," Shin said nudging the yokai, but he refused to move, then his companion joined him as well, laying down on the roof.

The song was growing stronger. Though she shouldn't, she turned around. The tree was right behind her as if they hadn't moved at all. Staring at it, her eyes began growing heavy. What was the point in even trying? The forest was home. It would welcome them into its arms.

"Akane, stay with me," Shin growled.

The few yokai who'd been following them had laid down and no amount of shaking would wake them. The rooftop disappeared and they were back in the courtyard. She was so sleepy. She wanted to join the others in their sleep. Grass had started to absorb the walls and vines crept up over her body as she laid down. Shin pawed at the vines, attempting to pull them off her, but they only wrapped around his body as well.

Shin roared with frustration and Akane closed her eyes. It felt like a few seconds when she heard a new song, a powerful song that seemed to echo through her and shook her entire body. It woke her with a start, and then she saw Hikaru running toward them, his eyes glowing green with power.

The grass receded, repelled by his song. Rin, just behind Hikaru, helped Shin and then Akane to their feet. As they stood vines fell away from their bodies. The other yokai were gone, nothing but lumps of grass.

"Looks like we came just in time," Rin said, looking around at the vines which were pulling everything toward the tree.

"Are you hurt?" Shin asked Akane, scanning her up and down.

"I'm fine," she said, shaking away the fog from her mind. That had been too close for comfort.

He pressed his head against her forehead, sighing in relief.

"We'll need to hurry. Hikaru can't hold this forever." Rin looked toward her husband whose arms were shaking.

Shin nodded his head before running toward the edge of the palace as they'd been before, but this time they were able to make progress. The gap between the palace and forest seemed enormous, but before they had to decide how to cross, Hikaru's song created a bridge of vines for them. They ran to the other side.

Just as they touched the forest floor, a loud crash echoed through the forest. Birds squawked in protest as they flew away. The echo of the explosion rippled through the forest as the walls of Akio's palace bent inward toward the tree.

When all the dust settled, all that remained was a massive tree growing out of the rubble, its white flowers glistening in shafts of sunlight.

"Everything has returned to how it's meant to be," the dragon said. She hadn't even noticed him standing there. He must have gone to find the priestess while they were escaping.

Shin looked at Akane, then back at the palace. Overhead a full moon rose. It was hard to believe almost a month had passed by. With everything that had happened, she'd nearly forgotten the kamigakari ceremony. A pool of dread settled at the bottom of her stomach.

"Tomoe! She was taken by the head priestess. We have to get to her before the ceremony."

She pulled away from Shin as if she'd run there alone. He grabbed her wrist to stop her from going.

"You're not going to do this alone. We'll do it together," he said.

He was right of course, if the head priestess had been pretending to be the kami all this time, she was going to need all the help she could get.

Twenty-Six

The day Mei had died replayed in Akane's head over and over. The head priestess had compelled her to kill her. For centuries, Akane thought herself chosen by the divine. Instead she'd been a guard dog for a malicious body thief. After explaining what she'd learned in Akio's palace, Rin and Hikaru had confirmed they'd encountered this body thief themselves. How had she not seen what the head priestess was from the start? Looking back now, she could see how different the girl who'd become the head priestess was from the woman she knew. The signs had been there all along, but she'd been blinded by her own beliefs and never realized.

Shin must have sensed her dark thoughts because he put his arm around her shoulder. "We're here now. We'll save her, don't worry." She leaned against him for a moment, taking comfort from his presence.

They stood outside the temple gates. A barrier shimmered around the perimeter of the shrine grounds. This was nothing new. During the ceremony, the priestess put their collective power together to protect the shrine from outsiders who could harm the kamigakari during her most vulnerable moment. Akane felt the prickle on her skin, the call of the kami, or that's what she'd always thought it was. But in truth, this was the head priestess' hidden power.

"We need to get through the barrier," Hikaru said as he examined it.

"Do you think together we can break it?" The flame priest-ess, Suzume, asked him.

Hikaru studied the shimmering exterior before nodding slowly. The two clasped hands and started to sing, their voices melding together until it was one resonating note. She glowing red and him glowing green, their combined power melding together, growing stronger together. The barrier around the temple started to wobble and shake.

"Go now," Shin instructed. Akane, bolted for the barrier as a gap opened up, Shin right on her heels.

The dragon and Rin were a few feet behind him when a competing song rose up from the depths of the temple. It clashed against Suzume and Hikaru's song. The discord of notes was a high-pitched screech that twisted inside Akane's skull. She stopped in her tracks to put her hands against her ears.

But just as quickly as it had risen, the sound faded, turning to a distant buzz. They searched for the source and discovered the barrier had closed once more. They were trapped inside. And outside the song was preventing Hikaru and Suzume from singing. The others were all kneeling on the ground and clutching their skulls.

They would have to continue on alone. They headed toward the shrine building. Outside every priestess of the temple, from acolyte to the highest-ranking priestess, knelt in lines, the more experience at the front, the less so toward the back. Each one was eerily still as they sang together. The air prickled with power that rose the small hairs at the back of her neck. Shin examined them with a tilt of his head.

He waved his hands in front of one of their faces, but the girl did not even blink.

"They're all like this," Shin said, standing up to face Akane.

"They're in a trance."

There was a stone in her stomach.

The doors to the shrine were closed, but when she grabbed hold of them they opened with ease. Tomoe was alone when she entered, seated before the altar, adorned like a bride on her wedding day. Decorative pins dangled from her coiffed hair. Bells on the end of the pins jingled faintly in the wind. For a moment, Akane was once more transported back to that horrible day. Mei's screams and the stench of smoke filled her nostrils. Shin reached out and squeezed her hand. Tomoe chanted along with the priestesses outside. She did not so much as lift her head as Akane approached.

Akane ran over to Tomoe, shaking her shoulders. "Tomoe, wake up."

The girl's blank eyes stared forward, transfixed on the altar in front of her. Smoke curled off the altar in lazy tendrils.

"Tomoe, come on, we have to get you out of here," Akane pleaded as she tried to drag her to her feet, but she felt like she weighed five hundred pounds.

"She will not be going anywhere," the head priestess said from behind them.

Akane spun around to face her, but with a flick of the head priestess' hand the door slammed shut, trapping her and Shin inside.

"What have you done to her?" Akane demanded.

The woman threw her head back and laughed. Her face was twisted, cruel, and there was a scar along her cheek, in the shape of a crescent moon that Akane had never noticed before.

"You surprised me, Akane, I never thought you strong enough to escape Akio. Though I suppose you had help." She looked at Shin who bared his teeth at her.

"Let Tomoe go, or I'll tear your throat out," she growled.

"You cannot stop me. I made you. I control you," the head priestess replied.

Akane transformed once more and rushed toward the head priestess but she merely held up her hand and Akane was frozen in place.

"It is too late; the ceremony has already begun. I have waited far too long for this moment to delay further. Obey me, and I will spare you."

"Then it was you. You made me kill Mei."

"Ah, her. I was close before with Mei, not perfect, but good enough. Until she discovered the truth, I had no choice but to eliminate her, and you were so willing to believe it was the kami's will." She smirked.

Summoned by her words, Akane's mind was filled with visions of Mei's death, fire and pain. Agony. Blood. So much blood. She fell onto the ground, trapped in her nightmares that would not end. Akane whimpered in pain.

"You don't control me." Shin growled as he lunged for the head priestess, but she caught him with an invisible hand in midair and dangled him above the ground.

"You should have taken my offer," she said before tossing him across the room where he slammed into the wall and fell into a lump on the ground.

The head priestess sang and it turned to screams in Akane's ears, Mei's screams pleading for her life as Akane took it from her. Everything was darkness, blood and fire.

"Kill him," the head priestess commanded, standing above Akane.

Akane stopped in place and growled as she tried to fight the impulse, while also pushing back the visions that threatened to overwhelm her. Shin was stunned, not moving. Akane stalked closer to him, fighting each step that brought her closer to him. Not again. She couldn't do it again.

Shin cracked open a golden eye and looked up at her in a daze. "Akane?"

"Get away," she growled between clenched teeth.

The head priestess' voice was urging inside her head. Demanding, invoking her animal nature, forcing her to do its bidding. Despite her warnings, Shin crept closer to her, his hand outstretched. She swiped at him, clawing his face, drawing blood.

The scent of blood was driving her mad, and coupled with the head priestess' command she couldn't control herself. She had to destroy him. She pounced on him, knocking Shin to the ground, now in full wolf form. She bared her teeth at him. But he wasn't long pinned beneath her. He transformed into a wolf and knocked her backward. They circled one another for a few moments. She snarled and lunged for him again but he dodged her and then went for her throat. Shin pinned her to the ground, only for a moment. She wriggled out from beneath him and caught him by the throat.

"You can fight it. Don't let her control you," he growled.

His golden eyes were trained on her. He did not struggle against her. One clamp of her jaws and she could end his life there. She blinked at him. Her memory was foggy. The last thing she remembered was someone calling out to her. The more she tried to think about it, the faster it slipped through her fingers.

"Finish him," the head priestess urged. And then she felt that pressure inside her skull.

But it was competing with her animal instincts, her logic, her reason, who she was. She wouldn't kill Shin. She knew who the real enemy was.

She forced Shin to the ground. "Play along," she whispered.

Shin lay on the ground, eyes closed and not moving. Akane turned to face the head priestess.

"Perhaps you're not as useless as I thought."

Akane stood before Shin, to block him from the head priestess' view. The old woman turned back to Tomoe where she stood on the altar, the incense rising up around her and haloing her head in smoke. She began to sing, the incantation that Akane once thought brought the kami into an earthly body. Very slowly as to not alert the head priestess, Akane crept closer.

The head priestess was focused on her incantation and did not notice her straight away. A bright aura was floating around Tomoe's body, a shimmering light. The head priestess raised up her hands, and in another second and it would be too late to save Tomoe.

Akane jumped toward the head priestess, intent to tear out her throat. Before she could reach her, the head priestess pivoted. Her hand held out in a stop motion, Akane froze in midair. The witch started to sing, her voice rising. Darkness poured out around her like thick black sludge. With a flick of her wrist, Akane was brought crashing to the ground. It flattened Akane to the ground, and the witch smirked in triumph.

"Did you really think you could defeat me?" She cackled.

A roar pierced through the priestess' song. The door burst apart in shards of paper and wood. Rin, in kitsune form, entered, her multiple flaming tails whipping around her.

The witch's eyes were wide with shock. "You—" she pointed at her.

"This is for Shin." Rin replied and opened her mouth. A blast of fire shot out and slammed into the witch, sending her flying backward into the altar, which tipped over.

The witch climbed up, blood running from a wound on her head.

"The two of you are not enough, I have gathered the power of priestesses for millennia. I am unstoppable—" Before she could finish her sentence, the roof started to shake and tremble. She looked up just as the roof was torn from the eaves, and the dragon in serpentine form hovered above them. A beam broken by the removal of the roof fell toward the head priestess.

Akane caught Tomoe by the collar, dragging her away, just in time to avoid the falling beam. She stood over the girl as debris rained down on her back and she cried out.

As the dust settled, Tomoe blinked and the glassy-eyed look in her eyes disappeared.

"Akane? What's going on?" she asked, looking around at the wreckage around them.

She sat up and pulled the girl into a fierce embrace. The dust settled and the group was left standing in the midst of the rubble. Shin rushed over to them.

"Are you hurt?" he asked.

She shook her head, and searched the wreckage. The priestesses outside were waking and looking around in confusion.

Tomoe screamed and pointed to their right. Lying under a pile of rubble was the broken body of the head priestess smashed beneath the fallen beam. Tomoe covered her mouth and then turned away from the destruction. Akane held her to her chest.

"It's over. Don't worry," Akane said, petting her head.

A disembodied laugh came from the wreckage. The beams slid back and the head priestess rose up. Her body was a torn mess of injuries. Her head was broken and lopsided.

"As I said, I am not so easily defeated."

Akane put herself between Tomoe and the head priestess. She rose up into the air, the black energy curling around her.

An arrow zoomed through the air, striking the head priestess in the heart. It glowed with green spiritual energy, which spread across the black, eating it away. A few feet away Hikaru lowered his weapon.

"Her power is weakened. If we can kill her physical body, she cannot return."

The head priestess came crashing once more to the ground. She stood, her head lolling to one side, her arms dangling uselessly at her side. Rin and the dragon rushed toward her, but her song propelled them backward.

Behind her Shin crept closer, but the witch picked up a piece of jagged wood and sent it flying, striking him hard in the shoulder and he fell to the ground.

"Shin," Akane cried out, before running toward the witch. Inside, her wolf howled, and Akane let go of all control of her wolf, giving into it. The power rolled through her, bursting out of her in an immense rush.

The witch turned toward her, just as Akane launched herself onto her, pinning her to the ground. Her eyes were wide as Akane's jaws clamped down around her throat, ending her life in a spray of blood. The last sounds she made were a strangled scream as Akane tore her apart.

TWENTY-SEVEN

Akane walked out into the early morning air. The brisk fall air felt good on her flushed skin. She tilted her head back to stare at the moon. What happened now? The temple was in shambles. The head priestess was dead. The kami was a fake. Most of these women had nowhere else they could go. This was home to them.

Tomoe had been resting in her room since the incident, and Akane had been too afraid to face her. She should have seen this from the beginning, should have known how dangerous the head priestess was and protected her from it. She'd almost died because of her.

Without realizing it, her feet had guided her back to the site of the former shrine. Nothing remained but a pile of rubble. The scent of blood still lingered on the air. Akane wrapped her arms tightly around her chest. She hated to kill, even someone as vile as the head priestess. Her death would be another mark upon Akane's heart. But if she'd been given the chance she would have done it again. If only she'd listened to Mei all those years ago, they could have run away together. But then the head priestess would have just as likely continued on as she was doing, and Akane never would have met Shin.

Orange and golden light rose up over the horizon. The sound of murmured voices approached from behind. Akane turned to see all of the priestesses filing toward the wreckage. They passed her by with hardly a glance, going to piles of broken wood and stone, gathering them up. Carrying them away.

"What are you doing?" Akane asked them.

Tohru stopped, her brows pulled together. "We're cleaning up."

"But why bother, the kami was a fake." Akane gestured toward the remains of the temple.

"We talked about it. Some of us wanted to leave. But Tomoe convinced us all to stay."

"Tomoe did?" Akane asked, scanning the crowd. She hadn't even noticed her mixed in with the other priest-esses, but she was struggling to carry a boulder away.

Akane rushed over, she took the boulder from Tomoe's hands.

"Why are you doing this?" Akane asked her.

Tomoe shrugged. "This is my home. Even if the kami isn't real. If you'll excuse me, I have more to clear away."

Akane shook her head with a smile, before joining the priestesses in their clean up. It wasn't long before, Shin arrived and without a word, he joined in by carrying a massive beam. He slung it over his shoulder, dragging it away. Then Hikaru showed up, picking up the other end. The two men stopped to look at one another before sharing a nod and continuing on with their work.

Rin brought water around for the working girls, and the flame priestess started a pyre to burn anything that couldn't be salvaged, while the dragon helped the other men carry heavy items away. Before long, the foundation of the old building remained, and night was falling once again.

The priestesses were coated in dust and grime, but they were smiling all the same as they headed off to their dormitories. Akane had worried they'd lose direction without the head priestess but it seemed she had doubted them. Just as she had doubted Tomoe.

Tomoe was the last to leave the site. Akane caught up with her, grabbing her gently by the arm.

"Can we talk?" she asked.

Tomoe's eyes were half-lidded. "I'm too tired for a lecture."

Akane shook her head. "It's not that. I'm proud of you. I think you'll be a good head priestess."

Her eyes flew open. "You mean that? There's a lot who are much older and more qualified…"

Akane rested her hand on Tomoe's shoulder. "I know you'll do great things. You'll make this temple greater than it was before."

Her smile broadened. "And what about you? Are you going to settle down with Shin?"

Akane flushed. Across the courtyard, Shin was waiting. She'd been putting off this conversation much too long.

"I suppose we'll see."

She said her goodbyes to Tomoe before jogging over to Shin across the courtyard.

"Take a walk with me?" he asked.

Akane nodded, her heart was in her throat. Even after she had pushed him away, he'd almost sacrificed himself for her.

Gravel crunched under their feet as they walked. Silvery moonlight peaked out from behind the white clouds. The sky overhead was an inky black. Shin's hand ghosted past hers. She ached for him to take her into his arms. But she didn't have the right to ask that of him.

"How are you feeling?" she asked. There had hardly been time to heal his wounds after his fight.

"I'm back to normal now. What about you?"

"Fine."

There was a faint smirk on his lips. "It's alright to not be."

Unexpected emotion tightened her throat. How did he know her so well? All day she'd kept her hands busy to avoid thinking about the head priestess. But now in the quiet moments of the evening, it all came crashing down on her again. Tears choked her words and she nodded. Shin pulled her close, enveloping her in his embrace. She rested her chin on his collar bone, inhaling the musky wolf scent of him. The smell untied the knots inside her as his gentle hand on the top of her head calmed her. She'd never been more grateful for him than in that moment.

"I worshiped her because she made me who I was. But she used me to kill Mei. She was wicked, but—" She sucked in a breath. "I loved her."

"It's not your fault," he soothed, his voice a hushed whisper.

"Where do I go from here? Who am I now?"

"That's the easy part, you can be whoever you want to be."

Was it? Perhaps for someone like Tomoe who knew she wanted to learn to fight. She would turn this shrine into a place for warrior priestesses to train. And she would grow into her power, guided by her fellow priestesses. Or someone like Shin, who had a place among his own kind. The dragon had already welcomed him back into the fold. For Akane, she had never been part of this world in the temple, but she didn't know how to be a yokai either.

She pulled away from Shin. She couldn't lean on him anymore, not if he had his own life to live. "I assume you'll be returning to the dragon's palace soon?"

"The dragon is impatient to return. There's something he needs my help with."

"That's great," she lied. Of course he wasn't going to ask her to stay with him. She'd already scorned him once.

"There's just one problem," Shin said.

"What's that?"

He grabbed her by the chin and tilted her head up to face him. "I don't know what your plans are." She inhaled sharply. A warm glow began spreading out from her gut.

She stared up into his golden eyes, his musky wolf scent surrounded her, and she ached to pull him closer. But she still held back. She was broken, and still feared yokai. But she wanted to learn more about who she was, what her dreams and hopes were outside of protecting others. She wanted to be a true wolf.

"And what if I say I'm not sure?" she whispered.

There was a familiar smirk on his lips. His breath fanned against her cheek.

"Then would you let me join you as you figure that out?"

She couldn't hold back anymore and leaned forward, pressing her lips against his. The soft yielding flesh opened up to her, letting her explore his hot mouth with her tongue while his hands bunched into the fabric on her back, bringing her close. Desperately, achingly, she needed him. To feel for once as if she was herself, as if she could regain a part of her that had been lost for so long. Once again, she was whole. She was an okami.

EPILOGUE

It had been hours since Shin had seen his mate. The dragon had kept him locked up in strategy meetings all morning. It had been hard enough tearing himself away from her that morning. Some days he woke up in her arms and couldn't believe how incredibly lucky he was to have her.

He was itching for another roll in the futon with her, but when he went to their chamber, it was empty. Not that he could expect her to lie around all day and wait for him. She'd found a role in the dragon's palace easy enough, helping with the training of soldiers and working as a liaison between the human and yokai gathering here.

He headed for the training grounds first and found Suzume and Hikaru training.

"Have you seen Akane?" he asked her.

The flame priestess shot a fiery ball at Hikaru who blocked it with a wall of earth that burst from the ground.

"I think she went out into the forest," Hikaru said.

Panic rippled through him. Though he was confident Akane could take care of herself, he couldn't help but worry. Danger seemed to be around every corner lately, and his position as the dragon's general put her at risk as well. He hurried out of the palace and into the forest beyond. He found her scent easily enough and followed it along the shore before it diverged into a wooded area just a few yards away.

He found her kneeling before a burial mound, hands pressed together in prayer. The grave was empty, but shortly after moving into the palace they'd erected it in Mei's memory. Partly to help Akane put to rest the ghosts of her past, but also to give her a place where she could talk to her when she needed to.

"I've found someone," Akane said to the mound, the words rang surprisingly raw. She hadn't sensed him standing there. It felt wrong to eavesdrop and yet he couldn't move away.

She inhaled and exhaled. "No matter how long I live, I won't forget you but I'm learning to forgive myself for what I did. I think you would want that, wouldn't you?"

He knew how she felt. They stayed up many nights, legs intertwined and talking about their pasts. Mei was carved into her heart in a way that Shin could never heal. And he didn't want to. Just as he didn't want her to make him forget about Rin or what he did for her.

The wind blew through the trees toward Akane. She'd likely catch his scent.

"Spying?" she asked without turning around, her voice teasing.

In his true form he approached her, golden eyes studying her. Akane smiled before transforming into a wolf as well and joining him. When she got close he bolted from her, leading her on a chase through the forest, across farmland, fields, and through tangled trees. At times she caught up, or even overtook him, then he'd take the lead once again.

They nipped playfully at one another and made quick turns, trying to throw the other one off track. They ran until they were both breathless. They fell back onto the soft grass panting and staring up at the blue sky. Fat white clouds drifted lazily across it.

Shin resumed his humanoid form as did Akane, and she laid down on his arm and curled in close to him.

"Will this kind of happiness last?" she asked as she nuzzled into his neck.

"Trying to get rid of me already?" he asked, teasing.

Akane covered her face with her arm, she pretended to block out the sun, but he knew it was to hide the tears that were threatening to fall.

"I can't help but worry about all the things that could go wrong. Tomoe and her temple, the dragon's war. What if you get hurt? What if I lose you? Or both of you? I couldn't stand it if I lost you both. Everything is so uncertain."

Shin leaned up on one arm, and caged her with his other arm, leaning over her. Her hair was undone and fanned out around her on the grass, she tried to avoid his gaze.

"I swear to you. I will never leave you."

He leaned down, pressing his lips to hers. Tears were rolling down her cheeks, but they were bittersweet.

"We've been through worse. Together we can do anything," she replied. And they both knew it was true.

Also by Nicolette Andrews

<u>Moonlight Dragon</u>

Empress Ascending (Newsletter Exclusive)

Dragon's Deception

Dragon's Temptation

<u>Thornwood Series</u>

Fairy Ring (Free)

Pricked by Thorns (Free)

Heart of Thorns

Tangled in Thorns

Blood and Thorns

<u>World of Akatsuki</u>

The Dragon Saga

The Priestess and the Dragon (Free)

The Sea Stone

The Song of the Wind

The Fractured Soul

The Immortal Vow

Tales of Akatsuki

Kitsune: A Little Mermaid Retelling (Free)

Yuki: A Snow White Retelling

Okami: A Little Red Riding Hood Retelling

<u>Diviner's World</u>

Duchess (Free)

Sorcerer (Free)

Diviner's Prophecy

Diviner's Curse

Diviner's Fate

Princess

<u>Witch of the Lake Series</u>

Feast of the Mother

Fate of the Demon

Fall of the Reaper

About the Author

Nicolette Andrews lives in San Diego with her husband, youngest child, cat and dog. A lover of rom-com K-Dramas, stabby heroines, and brooding heroes. She's best known for twisty-turny romantic fantasy and angsty plots. When she's not torturing her creations, she enjoys cooking, camping, and cozy videos games.

You can visit her at her website: www.nicoletteandrews.com or at these places:

facebook.com/nicandfantasy

twitter.com/nicandfantasy

instagram.com/nicolette_andrews

amazon.com/author/nicoletteandrews

bookbub.com/authors/nicolette-andrews

goodreads.com/nicolette_andrews

pinterest.com/Nicandfantasy

tiktok.com/@nicandfantasy